A German Family

COPYRIGHT 2021 by Nevin Schreiner

ISBN: 978-1-7361897-0-2

Disclaimer:
A German Family is a work of fiction. Its characters are not modeled on anyone, living or dead. They come purely from the author's imagination. Berlin is also imagined. The streets named here may or may not exist in the real city.

Book design: Mackie Osborne

Published by Burrow Books • Los Angeles, California

A German Family

Nevin Schreiner

 BURROW BOOKS

"I cannot prevent myself from reflecting that the Jews and their affairs bring bad luck on all who get too closely involved with them."

— Junius Annaenus Gallio
in Neropolis by Hubert Monteilhet

I

.1.

Heike met Frau Brest as Frau Brest was returning from Franz's Meat market and Heike was walking toward it. Heike smiled at her. Frau Brest nodded and told her to hurry, while he still had meat. Does he have potatoes? Heike asked. No. No potatoes, said Frau Brest, nodding for emphasis. Heike couldn't stand Frau Brest, but was always polite to her now. Her mother insisted. There was a rumor Frau Brest had informed on Herr Faber and no one wanted to be her next victim. Herr Faber had been cleared but he had come back pale and fearful, and now rarely left his apartment.

Heike ran the rest of the way to Franz's Fleischmarket. Inside, everything was cheerful and lit, in contrast to the gray, slippery streets. It smelled cold but good--the smell of vegetables and even meat, not of fire, burnt stone, cordite.

Taking her place in line, Heike smiled at a mother holding a three year old. It's still raining? the woman asked. Heike nodded. It just began. When I went out, it was sprinkling, but now it's raining hard. The woman shook her head and said, I thought it would hold off until evening like they said it would. They never get it right, an elderly man in front of them said. Sixty eight years, they get it wrong once a week. The line murmured, uneasily.

Finally, the woman in front of Heike stepped to the counter and handed the butcher her ration book. Franz, the butcher, nodded imperiously at the mother and, without changing expression, stuck out his tongue at the toddler, who began to cry. Franz then raised his eyebrows with comic dismay, causing those in line to laugh.

The toddler, Heike noticed, had strange hair, which seemed to grow down the center of his head. His eyes were almost blond, a half gray, half almond color. Heike wondered if she'd ever have children. She'd just found out where children came from and the news had filled her with horror. At first, she thought her friend Julia was making it up. But Julia insisted it was true and at last, Heike believed her. Horrible as it was to contemplate, Heike had determined to do it-- but only after she had grown up. She was thirteen. When she was twenty, or thirty, and had had enough time to absorb and come to grips with it, maybe she could take a pill and be unconscious while it happened. Heike's turn came and she stepped up to the display case where a very few cuts of meat glowed in the soft, freezing light Yes? said Franz, tilting up his chin. Cat got your tongue? Or do you want tongue? Franz exhibited what was left of a tongue. The customers laughed. Blushing, Heike handed Franz her ration book and pointed at a low pile of stew meat. Franz pulled the bloody paper container containing stew meat from the case, weighed out four ounces. Do I wrap the meat, or do you eat it here? Franz asked, squinting at Heike, who managed to croak out, Wrap it please, as the line dissolved in hysterics.

On the way home, Heike fantasized decapitating Franz and putting his stupid head in the meat case. A wet black cat ran across the street. Heike knelt and called to it but it wouldn't come. Heike loved animals and wanted one, even though they wouldn't be able to feed it. Many people had let their pets go. You saw cats everywhere but few dogs. Heike wondered where the dogs had gone and forgot about Franz.

When she got home, the front door to her apartment building was ajar so she didn't have to use her key. She had to urinate and gritted her teeth as she ran up the stairs. Maybe a rapist had opened the door and was waiting for her on the stairwell. She wouldn't be able to hold it in if he was. She would wet herself.

She rapped on their door and her mother opened it instantly. Heike ran in, dropped the package on the kitchen table, and slammed the bathroom door. Heike, her mother admonished. Heike didn't reply.

.2.

Frau Meitner watched her daughter disappear into the bathroom and sighed. Heike had become impossible. At least she had gotten something. Carefully, Frau Meitner unwrapped the package and examined the stew meat. There were tendons and gristle. But there was also a little marbling, which meant fat, and only a faint purplish tinge so the meat hadn't yet rotted. She would cook it tonight, after Hans came home.

She took the butcher paper, licked it clean, glanced guiltily about the kitchen to make certain no one had seen. Then she washed the paper and set it aside in the re-use pile. The toilet flushed and Heike emerged from the bathroom.

I had to go, she said.

Who was at the butcher's? asked Frau Meitner.

No one, said Heike and went into her room and closed the door.

Frau Meitner sighed and opened the secret drawer where she kept the potatoes. The drawer hid behind another drawer. She withdrew a softening potato and squeezed it, then withdrew a second potato, this one covered with eyes. She decided to use both. She took a paring knife from the utensil drawer, sat at the Formica table and began to peel the potatoes. She put the parings into a pot of water with other vegetable skins, to be made into soup.

When she was done, she rose, carried the potatoes to the sink and washed them. She dropped them into a pot of cold water so that they could revive. Once they had absorbed some water, they would lose their pulpy softness and she could cut them for stew. She dried her hands on a used dish cloth and returned to the table, where the meat lay in a small pool of red liquid at the bottom of the white casserole. Everything looked as it always had, she thought.

But some things were different. For one thing, Alfred wasn't there. There was no one to pester her at night after the children were asleep, or in the morning, before they awoke. She recalled him poking her in the small of her back as she tried to pretend she was asleep and almost heard him say, Pull it up, Trudi, meaning her night dress. The memory was so vivid, Frau Meitner said Not now aloud, forgetting he wasn't there. He might never come back. How would she feel if he didn't? Would she miss him? Did she miss him? There were some things she'd miss. She'd miss his taking out the garbage and changing light bulbs. He was good with his hands. But most men were....

Frau Meitner didn't allow herself to finish her thought. She rose and pushed the window shade aside to look at the sky. It was leaden. They would be able to turn on the lights tonight without fear of double checking the shades. If they had remained in their old apartment, they wouldn't have had to worry. It faced an air shaft. But once the Rosenfelds apartment became vacant, they abandoned their old place without a second thought. One morning, they were in the back of the building, on the sixth floor, the next, in front on the fourth.

Heike alone hadn't wanted to move to the Rosenfelds. She said they were dirty and no matter how much cleaning Frau Meitner did, their apartment would remain dirty. She'd had hysterics, flung herself on her bed and clutched the sides of her mattress, refusing to leave. They'd had to pull her off. Even then, she'd tried to run upstairs and hadn't calmed down until Frau Meitner gave her a drink of schnapps from their last bottle, forced it on her actually. Now Heike loved their new apartment. She was overjoyed to have her own room. She spent all her time in it. Frau Meitner had to yell to get her to come out.

Hans opened the front door, startling Frau Meitner. He grunted Hi Mutti, dropped his wet raincoat over the back of a chair and disappeared into the bathroom. Since he slept in the living room, he claimed the bathroom for his own whenever he needed privacy. At fifteen, he needed it all the time.

What's for dinner, he called, again breaking into her train of thought.

Beef stew, Frau Meitner said and waited. Her heart broke a little. He had been a sweet little boy, blond, blue eyed, with a shy, startled expression. He had buried his head in her lap whenever anyone spoke to him. She could remember him crying when Frau Wartheim stopped him on the street and asked for his name.

Frau Meitner rose and brought the casserole to the sink. If only she had an onion. Normally, she would begin with an onion, cut into thick rounds sautéed in rendered pork fat.

Then add four peeled and diced carrots, two stalks of celery and, a pinch of salt and four grinds of fresh pepper. Once the vegetables softened, you add one half cup of red wine and wait until the wine boils off before lowering the heat to simmer. The meat you braise in a separate pan until it is brown on all sides, using one teaspoon of duck fat to augment its own. Then add several whole cloves of garlic, which would be discarded after the braising. By discarded, of course, is meant stored away for another dish. Then the meat and quartered potatoes would be added to the simmering casserole along with spices such as sage and tarragon, and the whole would be sealed and allowed to cook until the juices from the stew meat are absorbed by the vegetables. The meat solids can then be used to make an au jus gravy, to be poured over the dish before it is brought to the table.

Those days were long gone. Now they were lucky to get meat one day in ten, lucky if the meat was edible. Tonight it was. Meat and two potatoes. A bit of rendered pork fat she'd been saving. A touch of salt. Hans and Heike would be drawn from their rooms by the smell. Trudi relished the thought of the family, minus Alfred, in the kitchen, absorbed in the petty tasks of life while she cooked.

.3.

Hans washed his hands and looked at himself in the mirror for a moment before lifting his pants and securing them with the belt. A curious, spitting sound drifted in from the kitchen. His mother was making stew. Where had she gotten meat? This was something Hans should look into. First it was necessary to wash his hands. Wait. He'd already washed them. How stupid of him. Maybe it was true that masturbation softened your brain. That alone, however, would not prevent him from doing it. The images he these days habitually conjured up of Frau Unger, white underpants at her ankles, hands flat on the mattress of her marital bed, her white behind facing him, were too stirring to resist. Even now, seconds after he'd achieved climax, they caused his member to stir. Not that, before she was sent away, Frau Unger had ever actually done, in real life, what Hans had her do over and over again in the Meitner bathroom. He might have been shocked if she had. In fact, their dealings had always been civil, confined to polite hello's on the stairs.

Hans stole a last look at the mirror, where his reflection brimmed with blond good health, then opened the bathroom door and stepped into the hall. Small, inarticulate sounds were coming from Heike's bedroom and Hans wondered if Heike too was masturbating. If she was, he would have to report her. Female masturbation was forbidden, especially in young women of child bearing age. Hans wasn't totally certain this applied to Heike. She was thirteen, but some things had to happen before a girl could bear children. He wasn't completely confident on this score, just fairly confident.

Tiptoeing to Heike's door, Hans stood outside and listened. The noises continued, interspersed with low, murmured words he couldn't make out. Then a squeal and a low moan. Hans placed his hand on the doorknob and turned. The door gave and Hans peered through the crack. His sister was sitting on her bed carrying on an imaginary conversation between two dolls she would alternately sail in the air, sit beside her on the bed, or mash together in an embrace. She was too absorbed to notice the door had opened so Hans closed it as quietly as possible and walked to the kitchen where his mother stood at the stove, her back to him. Taking advantage of her position, he lifted his chair from its place at the Formica table, placed it quietly on the floor, sat, and assumed a posture which suggested he had been there for some time.

Ach, Frau Meitner said, turning and putting her hand on her heart, you startled me. How long have you been there? One hour, said Hans. You scared me, liebschen, said Frau Meitner, coming up and ruffling his hair. Hans hated to have his hair ruffled but said nothing. Rain continued to drum against the window and Frau Meitner, getting the spatula from the third drawer, thought how nice it was, how like home-- she making stew, rain pounding against the window and Hans sitting, in his uniform, like a young god.

.4.

One floor up, Rolph Heinrich also sat at a kitchen table, this one covered with official looking documents bearing the state stamp of Schwabia, where his parents, and his parents' parents, had been born. Among the papers, one Rolph had been staring at for some time now was either a copy, or the original, of a document confirming his great grandfather's acceptance into the Lutheran faith. It could be nothing, no more than the legal record of Grandfather Steingardt's change from Catholicism to the family faith. Yet it could also mark his great grandfather's conversion from Judaism. Rolph had only to turn the paper over to find out which.

At forty-one and healthy, Rolph should by rights have been in the Wehrmacht, but his degree in fluid mechanics found him instead in a top secret, Berlin based rocket program, a program so secret few people knew it existed. His work meant that Rolph was one of only two younger men still living in his apartment building, the other, Stein Fassleheffer, being clinically insane. Rolph bore his odd status as best he could. As the war dragged on, and the younger men disappeared, more and more women looked at him with undisguised interest. Yet in many of their glances, Rolph felt, as well as in the expressions of all the older men in his building, there was a tinge of contempt. There was no apparent physical reason Rolph should be exempt from the war, no reason at all, except that what he was doing might help them win it.

Moreover, however much he might want to at times, Rolph could never explain his situation. It would have cost him his freedom, perhaps even his life, to divulge the mere existence of the rocket project. Not to Trudi Meitner, with whom he spent Tuesday and Thursday afternoons engulfed in carnal intimacy more profound than any he had previously encountered not to his daughter, who was away at Youth Camp. Certainly not to Steffi, his ex-wife. Were an acquaintance to see Rolph exit the number 81 tram at Beschloss Strasse one morning and then furtively enter a Mercedes limousine with smoked windows parked directly across from it, he was to say the person wasn't him. If the acquaintance insisted, Rolph was to intimate he was having an affair and then report the friend to the SA. If the person, still unsatisfied with Rolph's explanation then made the mistake of going to the SA himself, that person might disappear.

Taking a deep breath, Rolph turned the document right side up. For a moment, the gothic letters clumped together and he could distinguish nothing. As they gradually swam into focus, Rolph, who could hear his own heartbeat, saw his worst fears realized: his maternal great grandfather, Halder Steingardt, age 38, had converted to the Lutheran faith willingly and without coercion, thereby renouncing Judaism. Rolph had only the dimmest memory of Halder from a sepia photograph his mother kept on their mantel. He looked stern, but blond. His eyes were light colored and there was nothing in his face or bearing which suggested he was, or had been, a Jew. On the contrary, he appeared faintly forbidding, as though there were something military in his background. Rolph remembered being afraid of him.

Yet here he was, having converted. Documents didn't lie. Rolph looked up at the yellow kitchen walls, now lit by the single light bulb permitted after four o'clock in the afternoon. The outcome of this conversion could, Rolph told himself, amount to nothing. Suppose for example Halder's mother had been a Jew but his father was Catholic, or already a Lutheran. That would mean he, Rolph, would be one thirty second Jew, which would put him under the legal limit. Surely, if he put his mind to it, he could determine whether his maternal great great grandfather had had Jewish blood. He could direct an Inquiry to the State Census Bureau, which contained genealogies of every citizen born in Schwabia since 1500. But this, Rolph realized, might further rouse suspicion. What would be the purpose of his inquiry? And what would the inquiry be? A request for still more documents? Besides, the work he did was irreplaceable. Would they actually…

Rapping on his front door startled Rolph. Deciding the knock was too light to be the Gestapo, Rolph slid the conversion document back into its leather case, and called out, "Who is it?"

It's me, a soft female voice replied, carrying a hint of resentment.

Oh, Rolph said. Yes. I forgot what time… He unlocked the door and Trudi Meitner slid past, trailing a scent of violet water.

I have only twenty minutes, she said, turning to be embraced, because I'm making stew. Immediately aroused, Rolph reached for her even as she was stepping out of her blue checked house dress. A few seconds ago, he would have thought it inconceivable that he could achieve a state of arousal in his current mood, yet here it was, as always, pushing aside everything in its way. Putting his tongue in her mouth, Rolph reached for the light switch with his left hand. Trudi liked it to be dark when they made love. She made a sound with her full mouth and Rolph, without withdrawing his tongue, bent with her as she stooped to remove her shoes. He began to grope at the eye hooks of her brassiere, frantic to get it off. She pulled away, said hush, and took it off herself, then stepped out of her underpants. Breathing heavily, she turned and gripped the edges of the wooden table Rolph had inherited from his paternal grandfather, and emitted a slight gasp as he entered her from behind.

.5.

Ten minutes later, lying side by side on the kitchen floor, on which he had spread a blanket, Rolph couldn't make up his mind whether or not to tell her about the conversion document.

What is it? Trudi asked, responding to the character of his silence.

Nothing, Rolph said. I'm sorry you have to leave so soon.

So am I, said Trudi. Perhaps we can see one other over the weekend. Hans will be at festschrift.

Rolph who couldn't stand Hans kept his face neutral as Trudi turned rolled from him and stood and began to retrieve her clothes. Unselfconscious as she was about her body when they were making love, she always dressed in the bathroom, even after he had asked her, numerous times, to let him watch as she put on her bra and pants, garter belt and stockings, dress and shoes. She said it made her feel like a whore. But that would be how you should feel taking them off, no? Rolph would counter. Trudi would only shake her head and make her way to the bathroom.

The door closed and Rolph continued to lie on the floor, peering down at his own nakedness. Fortunately, he was uncircumcised. In the old days, that would have been conclusive. But now that there were biological standards by which one determined race, circumcision or the lack thereof was no longer a deciding factor. Take Edgar Rosenberg, who had been a fifth generation Lutheran and joined the party in 1937. His loyalty to the cause and his history as a Protestant didn't save him. In Rolph's opinion, it should have. If you were consistent, you would acknowledge that a hundred years of being one thing meant that you were that thing. But this of course, Rolph himself countered, as he heard pipes clang in the bathroom, was if you were simply being sentimental. In the old days, being a Jew may have been a matter of disposition. For the past four years, however, it was a biologically determined infection, which could be identified with complete precision simply by constructing an accurate family tree. Rosenberg's great grandmother and great grandfather had been Jews, and his maternal grandmother had been half Jew. Which meant

Rosenberg was one thirteenth Jew, and therefore, infected. He had to be removed from the body politic in order that... That what? That he not infect others? He could only do that by having children, which was why they too had been removed. But they were only one twenty sixth Jew, so they probably weren't sent where it was rumored...

The clanging stopped and Rolph shivered. Once night fell, temperatures dropped dramatically and the heat would only come on after the air raid, so as not to have a lighted furnace in the basement in case a bomb fell on their building. The superintendent of the building, Herr Strauss, had been a Jew. Not a rich Jew. A working Jew. There were working Jews. Not all of them had money. Not all of them, for that matter, had anything. Some were tall, blond, blue eyed, with wide shoulders and small ears. They looked for all the world like Aryans. Others, true, were short, overweight, pasty skinned. Some of the women had the pthistic quality of people who had never gone outside. But some Jewesses were very attractive, even blondly attractive. You could explain that, the biologists said, by Nature's tendency to provide each creature with protective coloration. As time went on, the Jew began to assume the outward appearance of the Aryan in an attempt to conceal from Aryans the trait that would eventually undermine all Aryanism. Before the present regime, the inability to be certain about who was or was not a Jew prevented the State from formulating a consistent policy. But now that every-thing was clear, that policy had been formed and was being implemented.

The bathroom door opened and Trudi emerged, dressed, but in her stockinged feet. She sat on a chair to put on her shoes and again, Rolph wrestled with himself whether to tell her. But tell her what? That he might be one sixteenth Jewish? The words themselves were absurd. Which sixteenth? His penis? Was that even a sixteenth? More like a thirty second, or a sixty fourth. His head? His head was...

So, Trudi said, I will send you a note about the weekend.

Good, said Rolph.

You shouldn't lie there, Trudi said, standing. You should get dressed.

Why? Rolph asked. Are you tempted?

Trudi shook her head. I must go, she said.

Rolph nodded and watched her disappear out the front door. They had long ago agreed she should let herself out in case neighbors were present on the landing. She could say she was looking after something in his apartment while he was away. Neither had the slightest illusion the neighbors would believe her. But neither would the neighbors, except for Frau Brest, challenge her veracity. Live and let live, they thought, unless your life jeopardized mine.

Rolph rose and, taking a fresh, stiff, cotton towel from his closet, made his way to the bathroom. As usual, Trudi hadn't flushed the toilet and her light yellow urine lay diluted in the water of the toilet bowl. Normally, there was something touching about this, a sign of intimacy, as well as of girlish forgetfulness. But today, with Jews forbidden to use the same public toilets as Aryans, at least when there still were Jews to use them, the sight of Trudi's urine in the toilet bowl filled Rolph with...with what? Dread? Fear? Not disgust, but a sense of disquiet. Is a Jew's urine different from an Aryan's? He'd spent forty one years thinking his urine was that of a full blooded German only to find that it might actually be Jewish urine...if not purely Jewish at least legally so. In which case, he shouldn't use his own toilet.

Rolph turned on the shower and stepped in. The cool, then warm water felt honest, soothing, calming, and Rolph, as the water grew warmer, pointed his penis at the drain and let go.

.6.

There followed two solid weeks of rain. Each morning of that two weeks, Heike awoke and immediately bolted to her window. She would go to sleep praying for rain. And for fourteen mornings, her prayers were answered. She never told anyone about the prayers. Hans was an atheist. And a young party member. He would have mocked her. Even reported her. Although Heike doubted this. He pretended to have contempt for her. But she had caught him spying on her while she undressed and Hans had begged her not tell their mother.

Heike didn't mind that Hans spied on her, but she couldn't understand why. She didn't hate her body. But she didn't like it either. It had begun to sprout two bulges where her breasts would be. They were soft and spongy and she enjoyed pushing them and watching them spring back to their original shape. Heike would have preferred to go on without them but knew she couldn't. They were there to stay. So was the dusting of hair that had sprouted around her thing. That was more troubling. She wanted to ask Mutti about it but Mutti was preoccupied. Whatever Heike asked her these days, Mutti said "Later."

In retrospect, the rainy days passed all too quickly. There was school. Always. And after school. There were occasional visits to her best friend, Julia, whose family lived one street over. And even rarer encounters with Frau Engstahl, who lived on the fifth floor and would sometimes invite Heike to have ersatz tea. Frau Engstahl was young and very beautiful. Her husband, she told Heike, had died fighting on the Eastern Front. Heike had only the dimmest idea where this was but she was sure their forces would win. She tried to reassure Frau Engstahl that her husband hadn't died in vain, but Frau Engstahl would only smile and stroke her cheek, or her hair. Heike was a little bit in love with Frau Engstahl and let her.

Heike also wanted to ask Frau Engstahl about whether Julia was correct about the procedure of conceiving and having children. But she was shy. Each time she nerved herself to pop the question, something would forestall it. Frau Engstahl would look sad, or else, so beautiful it took Heike's breath away. Or Heike would simply lose her nerve. Sitting across from Frau

Engstahl, a cup of warm tea in her hands, although it wasn't tea, it was just flavored water, Heike would feel the question rise to her lips. Frau Engstahl, is it true? she would hear herself begin. But was what true? That they put their thing inside you? She couldn't imagine herself ever saying this. How would it get in there for one thing? It was too soft and wiggly to go anywhere. Julia said it got hard as a rock but here, Heike was sure she was exaggerating. How could something that was that soft and small, she had seen Hans's when he was a boy, get that hard, hard enough to...? Especially if you kept your legs closed, which Heike was determined to do.

Besides, Heike told herself, Frau Engstahl didn't have children. Her husband had been called up just after they were married. Maybe she'd never had it done to her. And there were some questions you didn't ask people. For example, you never asked where their ancestors came from. You never asked about people who'd disappeared. The Knippers who'd lived on the top floor vanished one day. You learned not to mention it. You could ask your mother, or Hans. But no one else. Why not? Heike had asked her mother. Because I said so, Frau Meitner had replied, somewhat angrily.

What did I do? Heike asked, growing angry herself.

Nothing, Frau Meitner said, Don't make me angry.

All I did was ask where they went, Heike objected.

It's none of your business, her mother had said. And never ask Frau Engstahl. Ask me.

Okay, said Heike, then where did they go?

I told you. It's none of your business, shouted Trudi, red in the face. Now go to your room and be quiet!

Heike had gone to Hans's room instead. He was ironing his Hitler Youth shirt, using the top of his dresser as an ironing board. Where did the Knippers go? Heike asked. Hans continued to iron for a moment, then put the iron in its cradle and looked at her with unusual directness.

Do you believe in the Fuhrer, he asked.

Yes, she said, knowing that this was the answer Hans expected. The Knippers were Jews, Hans said. They were contaminated. If you had a roach in your apartment, what would you do with it?

I don't know, said Heike.

You'd kill it, Hans continued. If you weren't stupid, you'd... stupid or cowardly...If you weren't stupid or cowardly, you'd kill it.

What does a roach have to do with the Knippers? Heike asked, genuinely puzzled.

Hans had forgotten all about her. You may not want to kill the roach, he went on, talking to himself now. You may even feel sorry for it. But a roach is our enemy. You can't allow a roach to live with you. If you do, it will give birth to other roaches and soon it will take over your apartment. It will begin to eat your food, sleep in your bed. Before long, it will want YOU to leave. It will challenge YOUR right to live there. It will want YOU dead.

Heike had gone into her room and lain down. The Knippers were strange looking. They looked like they smelled bad. But they didn't look like roaches. They didn't even look like the people in the posters Heike paid no attention to in the streets. Heike picked up Polly, her number one doll, and began to comb her hair. Outside, rain beat against the window. It was only day 3 of the 14 days, though Heike didn't know that at the time. Her room felt dark and cozy, even though it was 9 am, Saturday. No school. She might see Julia, if the rain let up. They could talk about their dolls. Or they could talk about boys. There was a boy in Julia's apartment building who loved Julia. Franz. He was twelve too. He had very thick eyebrows. Julia liked him but she wasn't sure if she loved him. He kept wanting to hold hands but, so far, Julia had said No.

Boys, Heike said to herself, were stupid, but frightening. Hans had been a boy. Now he was something else.

.7.

Then one day, the rain stopped. There were still clouds. Wind blew the clouds over the gray rooftops. But the rain itself had stopped. Heike leaned out and looked at the street below. Here and there, patches of concrete showed under the puddles. The street was drying out. There might even be sun.

Heike's spirits rose. Sun. She hadn't seen it for so long. Ages it seemed. Ages and ages. Heike ran out of her room, getting to the bathroom before Hans got there. She closed the door and looked at herself in the mirror. Her braids had begun to loosen. She touched one. It felt soft, pliant. Mutti would have to do the braids up again, after Heike's weekly bath. There was knocking at the door. I'm in here, Heike said. Hurry up, I have to leave, Hans said. Heike waited to hear him go away before sitting down to pee. But he didn't. So Heike sat on the cold toilet seat and listened as the stream of pee hit the water.

Sun. A drop of sun fell through an empty patch on the frosted window. It landed on the tile floor and stayed there. Heike reached over and put her finger in the sunlight, watching the shadow crease the floor.

Hurry up and get done, Hans yelled. Heike wiped herself and flushed. Tonight she might be dead. The bombers could score a direct hit on their building and cave in the roof. The upper stories would fall into the lower ones, and they, in turn, would fall into the basement and crush everyone who'd taken shelter there. Heike pictured herself prone on the concrete floor, one arm thrown out in supplication, the other curled just under her mouth as if about to receive a kiss. The picture of herself lying dead on the floor made tears spring to her eyes. So young. So much to live for.

Hans began to pound on the door with his fist and Heike, frightened, quickly washed her hands, threw open the door, and darted past him. Her mother was calling from the kitchen that breakfast was ready. Sun was streaming through the apartment windows.

.8.

Because the the bathroom had become such an essential part of Hans's adolescent life, it infuriated him when Heike, or his mother, hogged it, which, in his opinion, was what women did with bathrooms. Whatever happened in there, there was no reason it should take as long as it did. When he wasn't masturbating, Hans could be out in three minutes. Less. Whereas they never took fewer than ten or fifteen minutes, no matter why they went in in the first place.

Once he finished his toilette, Hans returned to his room to dress. Mutti was under orders to press everything but his shirt the night before so that Hans could be assured of looking and feeling crisp for each new day. The black shirt he wore under his jacket sometimes he would press, and sometimes Mutti. The tie didn't need pressing. The boots Hans always polished himself. They were too important to be left to someone else, even someone as reliable as his mother.

Dressed and polished, Hans left the bedroom, accepted the kiss his mother ritually bestowed on him, tolerated her injunction to be careful riding his bike, and went out. The day was quickly warming up. Hans, who liked cool weather, nonetheless felt a surge of animal spirits at the caress of sunlight. After so many days of rain, the warmth on the back of his neck felt like a caress, though the image embarrassed him. Hans reacted to his embarrassment by riding faster than usual, taking turns at high speed, caroming out of skid after skid as if the Devil himself were after him. Only as he approached Dichter Strasse did he slacken up, worried that one of the Instructors might reproach him with reckless driving.

Fritz was already there when Hans pulled up to 123 Dichter. You're early, Hans said.

There's a selection. I come early for selections, said Fritz.

So do I, said Hans, but not as early as you.

That's because you're one of the chosen, said Fritz. Those of us who are not the chosen must make an additional effort.

Chosen for what? Hans said, secretly pleased.

For sacrifice, Fritz said. At 17, Fritz was among the older candidates. He had been kept from the front by a chronic case of asthma and would have been exempted from Service altogether if his family hadn't persuaded his mother's father, General Sheindler, to intervene. Even so, Fritz remained at the back of the class and was systematically ignored whenever it came time for assignments.

What are they selecting for? Hans asked as the two boys mounted the stairs into the undistinguished brick building that housed their Cadre.

I have no further information, Fritz said, pedantically. No doubt we will soon find out.

Hans said nothing. Two years of training had taught him to curb impatience. When the Instructors wanted them to know something, they would tell them.

Fritz was first into the classroom which, to the boys dismay, was empty. On the blackboard was a large chalked note instructing all students to repair to the auditorium.

Uh oh, said Fritz, I was afraid of this.

Of what? asked Hans. Fritz shook his head and picked up the pace, his rubber soled shoes squeaking on the highly polished, marble floors. No, of what? Hans insisted.

They're making a general selection, Fritz whispered, which could only mean they're assembling squadrons for the front.

What are you afraid of? asked Hans, a step behind. This is what we're here for, to defend our Fatherland. Fritz nodded, grinning in such a way that Hans couldn't tell whether he agreed or disagreed. Fritz opened the door to the auditorium and strode in, not allowing Hans to go first. He found two empty seats near the back and took the one on the aisle, standing so that Hans could slide past and claim the seat to his right. Hans immediately assumed the erect sitting posture mandated for formal assemblies. Though the auditorium was full, Hans noted, it was perfectly silent. You couldn't even hear breathing.

A side door opened and two SS entered, followed by Oberleutnant Grieg. Two hundred H.J. stood and shouted, Heil Hitler, and Greig returned the salute with a somewhat preoccupied air. He strode to the lectern, the SS taking up positions on either side of him. Oblivious, Grieg reached down and poured a glass of water, then, donning a pair of rimless glasses, began to read from a prepared text.

Herr Oberleutnant, he began, It has come to our attention

that the algorithm governing German birthrate indicates a potentially severe period of contraction in the purest sectors of our population, particularly that historically classified as 100% Aryan. Although the Office of Race and Population has anticipated this contraction as an inevitable consequence of the current hostilities, the rate of decrease now exceeds acceptable limits. To replenish our population stream, and ensure succeeding generations are provided with sufficient, racially pure manpower to control and supervise the annexed territories, we authorize the selection of one hundred racially pure Youth for transport to Liebenswald effective tomorrow morning. They will remain at Liebenswald no more than one week, after which they will be returned to their home venue. Signed, Heil Hitler, Rudolph Kranz, Gauleiter, 1st Medical Corps.

As Grieg looked up from the document, the boys stirred in a wave that passed from one end of the auditorium to the other. Grieg waited for the restlessness to subside, then glanced at a second set of papers resting beside the first.

I will call the roll, said Grieg. If your name is called, Rise and collect your belongings. Abend, Sepp. Ablauf, Heinrich. Abbatter, Sepp. Hans watched as the boys whose names had been called rose slowly to their feet, knelt, lifted their rucksacks from beneath their chairs, and came once more to an upright position. Agfahrt, Werner. Anderer, Billy. Axel, Johan. They wore slightly abashed expressions, and manifested signs of discomfort under the gaze of their fellow Hitler Youth. This remained true as their numbers swelled into C's, D's, E's, and F's, and continued to be true even after Hans was called and the roll progressed far beyond the M's into R's, S's, and T's.

* * *

For Hans, the rest of the day passed in a blur. Even though he excelled, as always, in small arms and semi-automatic weapons fire, in one instance even putting up a perfect score, the entire day wore an air of unreality. He was about to leave home for a longer period than he had ever been gone before, and to visit a part of the Fatherland he had never seen-- a part distinguished by alpine meadows, mountains and pristine lakes. Hans had always wanted to visit the Liebenswald area. Yet now that a visit was imminent, he felt strangely averse, even apprehensive. This was unlike him, and Hans set himself against the feeling, steeling himself to appear as certain and impermeable as ever.

So, said Fritz, when the day was over and the two were retrieving their bicycles from the bicycle rack. You were chosen. Hans nodded without replying. I knew you would be. Once I saw them taking only the strongest and best looking, I knew they would call you, so I wasn't surprised. I knew they wouldn't call me, because of my asthma. I'm big and strong enough, I think, but the asthma stood in my way. There's no evidence it's contagious, of course, or even hereditary. Dr. Langauer told me in fact that they believe it's particular to each individual sufferer. But they couldn't take the chance. I wish I'd been chosen, however, Fritz continued, wheeling his bike without getting on. I think I could have contributed something.

You'll have a chance later on, Hans said, consolingly. Fritz's despair at missing the cut made his own election easier to tolerate. They probably want to see how we do before they widen the program. That's not the point, said Fritz. They don't want imperfections, and you know as well as I, that I carry an imperfection. Hans opened his mouth to protest but Fritz stopped him. Of course, I agree with them in principle. If I were making the decision, I wouldn't allow me to breed either.

Hans examined Fritz, whose long straight nose, thin lips, fluorescent blue eyes, streaked blond hair seemed to him the essence of everything they were fighting for, everything they wanted and aspired and hoped to be. Yet inside this perfect outer case was a flaw, an insignificant one in Hans's opinion, but nonetheless a flaw. If by some chance it was transmitted to another generation, that generation too would be flawed, and would, in turn, transmit the defect to generations down the line. Though the resultant progeny might appear perfect, possibly even more perfect (although Hans couldn't see how) than the specimen now walking beside him, internally, it would be compromised, and compromised where it could do the most damage.

Hans felt for his companion. The two had been friends since kindergarten and had expected to remain on the same path forever. Now they would be separated. True, the separation was

21

only temporary, and only for a week. Yet in another sense, the separation was as wide as the earth itself. At one pole stood Hans and those like him, determined by the authorities as fit to be the bearers of the future of their race. At the other pole stood Fritz, eased however gently and compassionately out of the gene pool which would carry the spore of future greatness to untold generations. The thought of the gulf which had been opened between them made Hans, who despite appearances had an extremely refined sense of the tragic, want to cry.

Well, this is me, said Fritz, waking Hans from his thoughts. Good luck.

You too, said Hans. Be alert for traitors.

I will be, said Fritz. Contact me when you return.

I will, said Hans. Heil Hitler.

Heil Hitler, said Fritz.

.9.

After supper, after he had explained to his mother he was leaving the following morning, and after she had cried and he had told her not to worry but hadn't told her the nature of his assignment which was strictly forbidden, Hans excused himself and walked out of the apartment, down the stairs, into the street. He turned left at the apothecary's into Vogelstrasse, then left again into Eisenstrasse. At 111 Eisenstrasse, he pushed a doorbell and waited. After a few moments, a female voice said, Who is it? Hans Meitner, Hans replied and the door buzzed open.

Hans entered the familiar, musty smelling lobby and began to ascend the stairs. He feared elevators. You might get stuck in an elevator. Suppose the power went off while you were inside and the car stopped. With no light, you would stand in space, hoping the steel cable was strong enough to support both the car and its counterweight until help arrived. Or the power came back on. The stairs were more reliable. They had borne thousands, hundreds of thousands of ascents without cracking. They would bear one more.

Frau Gibbler had already opened the door when Hans appeared on her landing. Is it true? she asked.

Hans nodded without asking how she'd found out.

Frau Gibbler looked at him with pity, then shook her head and called to Grussie to come out. Coming Mutti, Hans heard Grussie say. A moment later, Grussie appeared, wearing a tight red sweater over a woolen skirt. Her hair was done up in braids and her bright, normally cheerful face was unable to hide the redness in her eyes. She skipped to Hans and kissed him on the cheek, then took his hand and told her mother they would sit for a while in the living room. Frau Gibbler nodded and returned to washing the dinner dishes.

In the living room, Grussie took a seat on the couch and tapped the cushion next to her for Hans to sit. He did, feeling ill at ease, yet excited, as he always did when he was near her. Time and again, he asked himself why he never thought of Grussie while he was masturbating. And each time the answer was the same: he respected her too much. She might someday be his wife. He wanted their union, when it came, to be gentle and loving, informed by the deep spiritual connection he felt they had already forged.

So, Hans began...

Oh, Hans, I know, she said, not waiting for him to finish.

Are you nervous? Grussie continued, wringing her hands, which sat restlessly in her lap. I would be.

No, Hans said. My assignment isn't of that nature.

That nature? Grussie repeated, puzzled.

Hans looked around the dim, over furnished room, with its two velvet couches facing one another like two mimics. A statue of Beethoven occupied one of the side tables, Wagner, the other. The Gibblers loved opera. Grussie did too. She had tried to make Hans love it but Hans, while he respected Wagner, and was stirred by The Ride of Valkyrie, didn't have the patience to sit through five hours of what he considered ridiculous nonsense. Especially not now, when the real thing flared all around them. Why waste emotion on a fat soprano, a woman as big as and seductive as a piano, when there were Grussies in the world? Why worry about Tristan when there was the Fuhrer? About Wotan, when there was Stalin and the Jews?

I won't be in danger, Hans said at length, feeling the stiffness of his words. Grussie regarded him, her blue eyes wide with incomprehension. Her hands had stopped washing themselves and fluttered lightly in her lap. Hans wanted to grab and kiss them.

You won't be in danger, Hans? Grussie repeated. That's wonderful.

No, Hans said. I'll come back soon, as well.

Grussie clapped her hands together and held them, as if afraid of what they might do if she gave them free rein. Oh, Hans, how I prayed for this, she said.

Hans nodded. He could smell the shampoo she'd used to wash her hair, hair which glistened despite the lack of direct light. On Grussie's neck were a few stray tufts of brown hair she hadn't managed to braid. Hans wanted desperately to touch them. And he was in fact reaching toward Grussie's neck when Frau Gibbler appeared in the doorway.

Would either of you like a glass of tea? she asked. We have no milk but I saved two spoonsful of sugar.

Hans put his hand down and said, Yes, thank you, Frau

Gibbler. Grussie nodded and Frau Gibbler, smiling enigmatically, withdrew. Grussie, he said when he was certain she was out of earshot. I have to tell you something.

Yes, what? Grussie replied. Her father, a Standartfuhrer in the SS had been on the eastern front for a year now. For the first nine months, they'd received regular communications, then the letters became sporadic. Lately, they had stopped altogether. The rumors that the army was in full retreat and mail couldn't get through were all that kept the Gibblers from despair. But Grussie was terribly worried about her Papa, as she called him, and Hans suspected he was constantly on her mind.

Nothing, Hans said, thinking of Standartfuhrer Gibbler.

No. You have to tell me, Grussie insisted, again clasping his hands in hers. You have to. You can't tease me.

What Hans had been about to tell her was that he was being sent to Liebenswald to serve as a stallion for racially pure German farm girls. But the earnest way Grussie looked into his eyes, the vulnerability which she allowed herself to show, even when she was simply seated alongside him, made this impossible. He couldn't bring himself to tell her he would return without the virginity that had been the subject of so many discussions between the two of them as they resolved to remain pure until the war was over and they could get married. Hans had wanted to get married immediately, but Grussie urged him to wait until he returned and they could do as they liked without asking permission from their parents. Wait until the war is over, she'd said, and we're no longer children. I will be there for you no matter what.

What if I don't come back, Hans had said.

At this, Grussie had shook her head vigorously and continued to shake it, as if she could both see the future and control it. Nothing will happen to you, she said. I know it. Nothing will happen and you will come back and I will be here, waiting for your return.

Hans didn't agree but had no choice but to accede. If he was old enough to die, he felt, why wasn't he old enough to marry. True, perhaps Grussie, who did have a slight overbite, wasn't as perfect as certain other girls. But she had beautiful hair, a beautiful body, what Hans had seen of it, and a beautiful spirit. And he was sure of his feelings for her, certain he didn't and wouldn't want anyone else.

And yet, when she refused to marry him, in all honesty, Hans felt a certain relief. To marry necessarily meant to embark on sexual relations with your wife and something in Hans resisted this. Part of it, he knew, was that he placed her on a pedestal. Yet, another part had to do with Frau Unger. If he married Grussie, he would have put an end to his nightly visits to Frau Unger's bedroom, and all that these visits entailed. And there was more. His relationship with Frau Unger had cast sex in a different light, one that he would have been unable to introduce to a woman as pure and lovely and loving as Grussie. Did this mean that he needed Frau Unger, Hans sometimes wondered, vowing that if the answer was Yes, he would forgo any further dealings with her. Sometimes the answer was Yes, but he was unable to complete the second part of the equation

I wanted to say, Hans temporized, returning to an earlier point, that I would like you to wait for me, no matter what happens.

Were you even listening to me? Grussie cried. Didn't you just hear me say I would wait for you forever?.

And not doubt my love for you, he continued.

Grussie reddened and looked away, in tears. He had never spoken to her of love before in such an open way. I won't, she managed.

And know that whatever I do, I do for you and for Germany, he said, feeling slightly ridiculous but feeling it was important to say this nonetheless.

I know that, Hans, she said quietly, still looking away as tears streamed down her face. Frau Gibbler took this moment to return to the room bearing a tray containing tea and a plate of home-made cookies. Here you are, kinder, she said, placing the tray on a large, claw footed mahogany coffee table. Fresh tea.

She lifted the teapot and began to pour. Hans looked at his watch. It was time for the bombers to come, but there were still no sirens.

.10.

Upstairs, on Rolph's bed, Trudi sat with her knees together watching Rolph pace back and forth. As reluctant as she was to leave Heike alone in the apartment, she knew that, whether she was there or not, at the first hint of a siren Heike would be off and running to the shelter without waiting for her, Hans, or anyone else. Besides, Rolph had never issued such a direct appeal before. He said he had to see her in such a way that she couldn't ignore it.

I don't know what to do, Trudische, he was saying, using a diminutive she hated. Suppose I am technically a Jew, I'm risking your life by even telling you this. Is it possible we should no longer see one another? It could incriminate you if they ever found out.

Trudi looked straight ahead, thinking it was just like Rolph, whom she'd always considered weak, to tell her something neither of them could do anything about. Why couldn't he have kept his mouth shut like a normal person? Why drag her into useless deliberations that would have had nothing to do with her unless he told her about them?

…I'm not one, Trudi heard Rolph saying as she tuned back in. Even if my grandfather was a full Jew, it's unlikely anyone will dig so far back as I already have a high security clearance. Yes, and grandfather was a converted Lutheran. My parents were half Lutheran, half Catholic, and I was raised Lutheran although it's true we occasionally went to midnight Mass and Easter services with my mother and her sisters. For this reason, Trudi, it's unlikely I should ever come under suspicion from that quarter but I thought it best to warn you and give you the opportunity to think for yourself about whether you want us to continue to see one another.

At this particular moment, the last thing Trudi wanted was to spend another second in the room with Rolph, although not because of what he might be but rather because of who he was: a simpering weakling who couldn't leave well enough alone. For my part, he was saying, I feel like part of me would die if we could no longer see each other. If that comes into your calculations, know that from the bottom of my soul, I would like to continue seeing you. I know I'm contradicting myself, but I can't get a clear...I can't think clearly yet. I just know that I...

Afraid he was about to tell her he loved her, Trudi rose as rapidly as possible and moved toward the door. Let me think about this, she said. It's a lot for me to digest at one gulp.

Rolph nodded, pausing in mid stride and looking at the heavily curtained windows. It's strange, he said, that the bombers haven't come. The first clear day in weeks.

What? asked Trudi.

The first clear day since the 14th. They're expecting a large raid. But it's already after nine.

Trudi paused and nodded. This was true. The radio had warned everyone to prepare for a long stay in the shelters and announced that, for those who still had reception, state radio would broadcast Das Rheingold in its entirety, beginning at eight pm. It was now past nine, so they were one hour into the opera. Is that why you're in uniform? Trudi asked.

Rolph shook his head. I simply can't believe any part of me is Jewish, he said. It makes no sense. Any more than it would make sense if someone said part of me was a woman. Do you want to know what's truly ridiculous, what really drives me insane? I ask myself, Suppose this is true. That what a Jew feels like is what I feel like. Because I feel no different than I did before I opened grandfather's papers, that is, before I learned might be a Jew.

Why did you? Trudi asked.

Why did I what?

Open his papers, Trudi asked.

Rolph thought a moment. I'm? I...They had just come. I thought, this is my history, a history of my family's bloodline. I couldn't have known what I would find there.

I thought you said you'd requested the papers because you remembered your mother saying something about your grandfather converting.

Yes, that's true, Rolph admitted, sitting and holding his head in both hands. Yes, that was why they sent me the papers. I'd... Rolph broke off, confused. Then why did you ask me why I opened them if you knew what they sent them for? Who wouldn't have opened them?

Trudi stepped back into the room and sat on the edge of the

bed. Rolph was right. Why did she ask if she knew the answer. Because, she realized, that was not her real question. Her real question was, In spite of everything you've told me, why didn't you keep your mouth shut? Why burden both of us with this information? If you hadn't told me, and you were found out, I would have been able to answer, with complete honest, that I had no idea you were a Jew. I assumed, because of your looks and your last name and the fact you were still living in the building, and your work, that you were Aryan. Good. All right. I agree, I can still say these things with what I now know about you. But I won't be able to say them with the same innocent conviction. I'll have to simulate my conviction.

I realize this is hard for you, Rolph was saying. But honestly, Trudi, I feel we can get through this if we just stay together.

What?, she asked. Get through what?

Whatever lies ahead of us, Rolph said as sirens began to sound. Trudi sprang to her feet while Rolph walked quickly to the closet and retrieved his air raid warden's helmet. You go first, Rolph said. I'll follow.

Trudi nodded and strode to the door, hoping to make the stairs before Rolph's neighbors, who were nonetheless fully aware of her liaison, could see her. She had had a difficult day. First Hans. Now this. At least she was first onto the landing and was bolting down the stairs before any of the others emerged from their apartments. Far below, she thought she could hear the familiar rap a rap of Heike's footsteps as her daughter likewise sprinted toward the shelter.

The bombing would be a heavy one. Now that the British had targeted residential districts, no one could consider themselves immune. Each time the sirens went off, it could be your number that came up in her city's nightly lottery. This of course, Trudi ruminated, was why she had allowed herself to become involved with Rolph in the first place, a moral weakling whose prospective Jewishness, if true, would explain everything. If there had been no war and she had been single, Trudi would have been able to choose from a vast pool of male candidates. It was the war that made Rolph, if not attractive, at least convenient. That and the fact he was sexually appreciative and, she grudgingly admitted, an adequate lover. Adept even. He wasn't like her brutal husband who considered her body merely a means, and sometimes, even an obstacle, to his own pleasure. Rolph touched her as though she were a musical instrument. He knew each note her body could produce. He didn't go straight for her sex with his blunt fingers, then ram himself in as her husband did. Sex with Rolph was diminuendo moving gracefully toward crescendo. It had detours, pleasurable glissandos, thunderous tympani. At times, her orgasms took the top of her head off, something that had never happened to her before, not even when her husband pulled her hair.

The lower Trudi descended, the more crowded the stairwell became. It seemed as if the entire building was heading toward the cellar, conversing quietly or not at all, moving deliberately but without pushing or panic or untoward display of emotion. People greeted one another with wry smiles, shook their heads, offered older people a hand...behaved, in other words, as civilized Germans behaved. Except, of course, for Heiki, who was too young to be able to contain her emotions and so could be forgiven.

Inside the shelter, Trudi would find Heike and they would sit together. Someone would have brought a radio. They would listen to Das Rheingold and Heike, who, unlike Hans, loved opera, would fall asleep with her head in her mother's lap.

.11.

The shelter was still largely empty as Heike arrived and ran to the far wall, where she knew she would find elderly, arthritic Herr Gruber sitting on his cushion with his hearing aid in place, waiting to begin his count. Herr Gruber was named Gottfried, like her bear. Also like her bear, he was furry, even to the hair sticking out of his nose. Normally, this would have soured Heike on him forever, but he always brought a candy to the shelter and, besides, even though it would only be for a few minutes, Heike didn't like sitting alone.

She found Herr Gruber with his pant legs over the tops of his socks, his white shins looking like skinned weisswurst left too long in the refrigerator. Heike said Hello and quickly plopped herself beside him while he greeted her back with a smile.

They're early today, no? said Herr Gruber.

I ran, said Heike. Everyone else was walking.

Yes, said Herr Gruber, they can't wait to drop their bombs on us. That's what they're like, these Jews. They can't wait for anything.

It's the English who are bombing us, said Heike. That's what they told us in school.

Herr Gruber smiled and adjusted his pants. Heike's glance strayed to his crotch and caromed back again. Was it possible that even old men like Herr Gruber...? She didn't complete the thought. Of course it was possible, but so long as she ignored it, maybe it wasn't.

Jews can't wait for their change and they can't wait to drop bombs. Wait until we've taught them a lesson. Then they'll wait, Herr Gruber said, nodding to himself, his rheumy blue eyes twinkling as he placed a handkerchief on his knees. Reaching into his pocket, he then removed a small piece of chocolate and set it on the white fabric. Look what I brought for us, he exclaimed, smiling.

His teeth, Heike noted, were chipped and yellow. Thanking him, she wondered how old he was. He might be a hundred, but Mutti said he was probably only eighty. He looked a hundred. Heike slid the chocolate into her mouth. It tasted like fake raspberry, her favorite. She closed her eyes and let the raspberry flavor roll over her tongue. Bliss. For a moment, it even made her forget her fear. Then a child began to wail – the shelter was rapidly filling – and her peace was shattered. Heike had nothing against children but hated it when they cried. It was bad enough being in the shelter when everyone was calm.

They should have a separate shelter for children, Heike said.

Herr Gruber nodded in agreement. Yes, he said, the Fuhrer should have begun to rid us of Jews earlier. I am not blaming him, mind you. He alone had the courage to do what was necessary. But if they had let him do it earlier, they wouldn't be bombing us now.

Heike swallowed the last of the chocolate and watched as people walked by, claiming their habitual places. The Isseldorfs with their idiot son rushed past, carrying a set of blankets. Then Harald Krankstaff, and his mother and father, and his sister Brunhilde, and some other people Heike didn't know, and the Burgenfleisses and the Holderins, and more people she knew but she didn't know their names. There was Mutti, just coming off the stairs, carrying Gottfried. Heike had forgotten Gottfried but knew Mutti would remember. She always did.

And Hans. He was coming too, wearing his HJ uniform. He had probably been doing something in the bathroom when the sirens sounded. Heike shut her eyes tight and concentrated on the taste in her mouth. It was disappearing more quickly than she would have liked, but then again, it was a miracle Herr Gruber was able to get candy at all. She wondered how he did it.

As Mutti took a seat beside her, the first bomb fell and Herr Gruber, holding up a horny forefinger, counted One. Hans took a seat to Herr Gruber's left, leaving Heike sandwiched between Mutti and the old man. Two, said Herr Gruber triumphantly as a second bomb fell. The bombs sounded as though they were six or seven miles away. Heike had learned to tell their distance from Hans, who was an expert on bomb estimating. Three, four, five, said Herr Gruber. Good evening, Frau Meitner. Good evening, Herr Gruber, Mutti said. The Jews, Herr Gruber began, but interrupted himself to count six seven eight nine ten. People were hurrying now, impatient to get to their places as the bombs fell closer. Heike leaned into Mutti, who seemed distracted, and Mutti absent mindedly allowed her to take Gottfried out of her grip and clasp him to her chest. She felt better with Gottfried in her arms.

Fifteen, sixteen, seventeen, Herr Gruber said. A man across from them asked if someone could shut him up, but the man's wife shushed him and he turned away from them. As he did, Heike could see the man was missing an arm. He had probably been at the front, she speculated, hearing Herr Gruber enter the twenties.

Do you want something to eat? Mutti asked Hans. Hans shook his head, almost surly. You should eat, Mutti said. You might have to leave right after it's over.

But I am not hungry, Mutti, Hans said. Whenever Hans was angry, he talked like a professor, noted Heike. She licked her fingers, hoping to find a last taste of chocolate. Herr Gruber was staring at the ceiling. He had reached the thirties and now the bombs were clearly working their way toward their neighborhood. You could always tell when the bombs were receding. This time, they were coming closer, which meant the bombers were approaching Kreiskellen, their borough.

Everyone had grown silent. All you could hear was some children crying, or screaming, as their mothers tried to calm them. Heike glanced around the vast shelter. Half its occupants stared at the ceiling, as though they were somehow able to see what was happening through the concrete. The other half sat hunched over, holding their knees. These were mostly younger women and old men. There weren't many men since most had gone off to the front. There were a few younger ones, like the man who had lost an arm, and the upstairs neighbor who, in Heike's opinion, was probably being investigated for being a Jew. Mostly the men were over forty, and many, she felt, were over a hundred. For some reason, Heike had a sudden image of Franz the Butcher leering at her over his meat counter and wondered which shelter he was in. She hoped wherever it was, the bombers...No. You couldn't hope for that. Other people would be killed too.

Maybe he would be running from his store though and they would see him and drop a bomb that hit only him. Even this, Heike reminded herself, as Herr Gruber entered the fifties, was verboten. You couldn't wish death on anyone, so long as they were Aryan. That's what they taught you in school, along with how the Fuhrer had saved Germany and how hard he had struggled to keep Germany out of the war until the Jews made it impossible for him to preserve both peace and self-respect, not to mention the respect of others.

A report shook concrete dust from the ceiling and some of the older people began to cough. Everyone was now looking up. The lights flickered and, at the next explosion, went out. Flashlights began to dot the shelter, like fireflies. Another bomb, 68, fell nearby dislodging clouds of dust which wafted onto the shelter's occupants. Mutti put an arm around Heike and drew her close. Heike clutched Gottfried, and glanced at Hans, who was gritting his teeth. Herr Gruber had cupped his hand behind his ear and was waiting. Seventy, he recited. That was weird. He should have cupped his hand when the bombs were far away, not now, when...seventy one, Herr Gruber said a moment before the seventy first report, whose shock wave knocked him on his back, his white legs waving in the air. There was a lot of screaming, then silence, as people waited for seventy two... Of course there were more than seventy two bombs, but Heike liked to believe Herr Gruber's count was accurate.

The seventy second bomb deafened everyone. Some screaming broke out among the women, but, for a moment, all anyone could hear was the ringing in their ears. Men had sprung to their feet and were playing flashlights over the ceiling, which was partially obscured by falling concrete dust. As her hearing returned, Heike could hear shrieks of terror, some close by. She noticed Bruno Faschinger, who was in her class, crying silently. Or was he crying out loud but she couldn't hear him. Bruno saw her looking at him and turned away in fury. His mother already had two children in her arms and couldn't hold him too. Besides, he was too old to be a crybaby. He was eleven. He should be gripping his thing, the way boys did at recess, and not crying. If they were going to die, it would be in the next ten seconds, which Heike began to count off out loud.

Hush, said Mutti, but Heike ignored her...Six...five...four... three...two...one...

Nothing happened. Then there was a huge boom, but farther down the street, away from the Meitner apartment building. The bombers had passed. Bombs were now falling to the north, away from Kreiskellen. They had missed. They hadn't destroyed their apartment building or killed them.

* * *

Trudi felt someone tapping her on the shoulder but for a moment, couldn't imagine why. She knew she had Heike in a death grip and was terrified that when she released her, she would find a suffocated child. But Heike released herself and seemed fine. She was clutching her bear by the neck, but was otherwise herself.

The tapping persisted and Trudi turned to see Herr Gruber, who had righted himself without assistance but looked alarmed. Did I miss any? he asked. He looked different. Trudi realized his false teeth had fallen out. They must have fallen out when he fell down.

Hans, Trudi said, see if you can find Herr Gruber's teeth.

Did I get them all? Herr Gruber asked, his sibilants spraying a bit in his toothless mouth.

What? said Hans.

He lost his teeth. See if you can find them on the ground, Trudi said. Then, turning to Herr Gruber, No, you did fine. Wonderful. You counted every one, she said.

All around them, people were struggling to their feet. Trudi bent to help Herr Gruber. To her left, Hans knelt, combing the concrete floor with his flashlight. Are you all right, Herr Gruber? Trudi asked. The old man nodded, brushing himself off with his frozen, arthritic hands.

Here they are, said Hans. Someone give me a handkerchief.

Do you have a handkerchief, Herr Gruber? Trudi asked.

Herr Gruber patted himself, then handed her the handkerchief on which he had placed Heike's candy. Trudi passed the handkerchief to Hans, who then plucked Herr Gruber's wet teeth off the floor. He handed them to Herr Gruber, who accepted the teeth with a look of puzzlement, then said, Ja, and put them back in his mouth.

Let's get out of here, Hans said.

Trudi nodded and scanned the space for Heike, who must have gone ahead. Did Heike leave, she asked.

Yes, said Hans. Let's go.

Take Herr Gruber's arm. He's disoriented, said Trudi.

Hans took the old man's skinny arm and turned him toward the exit doors.

The lights still hadn't come on and the progress toward the exits was slow and difficult. People bumped against one other, sometimes producing cries of anger or hysteria. On the other side of the shelter, someone was wailing hysterically. This tended to happen more, now that the bombings were more frequent.

As they approached the stairway, Trudi could see a number of people drinking from flasks or bottles. Liquor was forbidden in the shelter, but the wardens tended to look the other way. Why not? Rolph had said, when Trudi questioned him about it. Why not let them drink. They just lived.

What do you mean? Trudi asked.

They've lived. They could have died but they didn't. So they've lived.

Seeing that Trudi was puzzled, Rolph continued. You see, Trudi, it's like sex. If you didn't know sex existed, you wouldn't know what you'd missed. You might have a dim idea, no? that you were missing something. But you wouldn't know what. You could only know what you have missed once you've had it.

This is a contradiction, Trudi objected. The people haven't died, so how could they know what they'd missed by being alive?

Rolph had smiled at her.

No, I'm quite serious, Trudi said. You have completely contradicted yourself. The people who might have missed knowing sex would have had to known it existed to miss it. But people can't die to miss being alive.

Rolph had laughed at this and Trudi remembered being so furious, she had begun to beat him around the head and chest. At first, Rolph simply protected himself. But when she persisted, he'd grabbed her wrists and pinned her to the bed. And one thing had led to another, and when he finally released her wrists, her dress was around her waist and he'd somehow found his way inside her and she'd somehow found a nonverbal way of telling him she wanted him to secure her wrists again. So he had.

That had concluded their argument, Trudi now remembered, amidst the general outpouring of relief. And she understood clearly, completely, with all her soul, what Rolph had meant.

36

II

.1.

It was a full day later, and snowing, when the train carrying Hans and his Hitler Youth cohort pulled into the quaint platform of the Liebenswald station, with the word LIEBENSWALD inscribed in old high German on the swinging wooden placard bolted to the bottom of the station's eave. Inside their warm compartments, Hans and the other boys passed suitcases down from the luggage racks, donned overcoats, or stood quietly, awaiting further instructions. Next to Hans stood Willi von Stauffenberg, one of the older boys in the cadre. Willi yawned deeply and offered Hans a cigarette which Hans declined.

Their winter clothes made the compartment feel even hotter and everyone was eager to exit the train. But you had to wait for orders. If everyone did whatever they liked, the result would be chaos.

At last, a Standartfuhrer appeared, wearing the black leather coat of the SS. With him were two avuncular, middle aged civilians in wool topcoats. The Standartfuhrer told the Hitler Youth to form ranks on the platform and where they would be given further instructions. Hurry up and wait, Willi said, grinning. Abruptly, Hans remembered that it was Willi who had said to bring nylons for the girls. Willi said the girls would like this and the boys would too. The feeling of skin next to nylon was extremely erotic. At this, Hans had walked away. They were going to Liebenswald, not a whorehouse, to meet young German women, not prostitutes, or women like Frau Unger, with whom you could do what you liked.

Once outside, Hans took a series of icy breaths, which invigorated him, but the wind soon became too much and he and the others had to turn their backs as they waited to be told what to do next. Hans allowed himself to lean into the wind, whose gusts were strong enough to support his weight. They were in the mountains now, where weather was the Fuhrer.

Soon a second SS materialized and addressed the boys through a megaphone. They were to pass through the station, to the road on the far side where busses awaited them. They were to board in the order they arrived, with or without their cadre. Cadres would reassemble once they reached camp.

The mass of Hitler Youth stirred, then began to move. Hans stood at attention until it was his turn, whereupon he fell into step with the youth in front of him, entering the warm, brightly lit station only to exit once more into the savage wind. One bus was just leaving and another pulling in to take its place. Hans ascended the snow-covered stairs into the long, dimly lit seating area and took a seat near the front. The sudden warmth made him shiver and his teeth chattered for a moment as cold seeped out of his clothes and shoes. Other Hitler Youth had mounted the stairs and were now making their way down the aisle. Each time a boy passed, he released a gust of ice cold air.

Hans was by the window and therefore had nothing to say when Willi von Stauffenberg lowered himself into the empty aisle seat. He was tempted to ask von Stauffenberg to sit elsewhere, but there was no reason to. True, Von Stauffenberg was irreverent and politically immature, but he was universally liked and admired by the HJ instructors for his skill in shooting and martial combat. Rumor had it he was from an aristocratic Bavarian family so Hans felt doubly shy of antagonizing him, doubly because of his innate reluctance to antagonize any fellow Hitler Youth.

This weather is fucked, huh? said Willi.

Hans smiled slightly but said nothing. He felt hyper sensitive from his sleepless night, and uneasy about what awaited them at Liebenswald. Throughout the bus trip to Liebenswald, images of his bombed street had fluttered unbidden into his consciousness: flames licking out of the glassless windows of apartment buildings three down from his; coils of fire rising from what used to be roofs; bricks, pieces of furniture, broken gargoyles forming a carpet on top of which dozens of canvas hoses slithered like snakes emerging from an underground hole. The images rose and fell unbidden, finally vanishing altogether at his first sight of the town of Liebenswald, whose immaculate cobblestone streets had been recently swept and were just beginning to accept a fresh coat of snow. The buildings, low two-story shops and residences, sported steep, quaint roofs, like fairy tale houses, an effect heightened by their windows being rhomboidal, or irregularly rectangular, or square on three sides but skewed on the fourth, anything in other words but normal. There were no people on the streets, but the town appeared welcoming nonetheless.

As the bus wound through Liebenswald proper, Hans's companions fell silent, as if the town had cast a spell on them. Willi, next to Hans, poked him once in the ribs to point at a polychrome crucifixion set into a niche of what appeared to be a local tavern. Hans nodded. The image of polychrome Christ, twisted on the cross, disturbed Hans and made him angry. He was afraid that if he replied to Willi, he would express his anger so he remained silent. Mixed metaphor, Willi said, and grinned. Hans also grinned, relieving some of the tension.

* * *

When Hans awoke a half hour later, the busses were stopped on a large circular drive in the midst of what appeared to be a resort camp. There was a huge common building, painted white, with a steeply canted roof supported by columns that ran the length of a wide unscreened porch. All the lights were on. To the left and right of the main building were other buildings, smaller, also painted white, also steeply roofed. Some of these were dark, others lit. Throughout the bus, boys were rising to their feet and Hans followed suit, feeling somehow that he'd entered a dream world. He was asleep on his feet and not certain that he wasn't dreaming.

The blast of frigid air that hit him in the face as he descended the bus convinced Hans he was awake. His feet disappeared into five inches of powdery snow and he shivered in the biting, whistling wind that found its way to every opening in his Hitler Youth overcoat. SS were shepherding the boys into the main hall. Hans quickly fell in and marched with others up the wide... very wide...wooden stairs into a high-ceilinged foyer, and from there into an enormous, and enormously high, hall lined with photographs of the Fuhrer, the Luftwaffe, the SS, the Imperial Eagle, various urban rallies, Heinrich Himmler, Liebenswald, the camp in its summer clothes, snd so forth. The highly polished floor reflected the light from numerous wall sconces while each window wore a small beard of snow, rising from the bottom sill. Grateful for the warmth, Hans allowed himself to be pushed into a horizontal row of unfamiliar looking Hitler Youth and waited, half asleep, for whatever would happen next.

A third Standartfuhrer appeared, this one about sixty, and the boys instantly grew quiet. The Standartfuhrer welcomed the boys and told them to pay attention as he was going to read out their dormitory assignments by unit. Once the assignments were read, the boys would be escorted to their respective dormitories where they could use the toilets, wash, and then come back to this hall for dinner. Those who did not wish to eat were free to remain in the dormitory until the camp assembly tomorrow morning at seven sharp. He concluded by saying Heil Hitler, to which the boys gave a rousing response.

* * *

As he sat on his bed in his dormitory, a huge Nazi flag hanging from the ceiling, Hans felt as though his spirit had been divided in two. On the one hand, he was all but committed to Grussie. He had no doubt he was in love with her and wanted nothing more than to return from the war, having done his duty, and commit himself to her for the remainder of his life. To Hans, Grussie represented everything that was noble about German womanhood. She was pretty, full bodied, clever, witty, naughtily submissive, dutiful, and chaste. On the other hand, however, Hans understood the necessity that had taken him and his fellow Hitler Youth to Liebenswald, even though he felt Liebenswald to be a waste of his real talents, which lay in strategy and warfare. Morally, Hans believed, it was wrong to have sexual relations with someone you didn't love, when circumstances forbade you to have them with someone you did love. He had to agree, however, that the needs of the Reich superceded those of any one individual. In order to function for the next thousand years, the Reich would have to count on a steady stream of pure Aryan stock, both to oversee the assimilation of those worthy of assimilation, and to govern or otherwise deal with those who required constant supervision. This was as plain as the nose on his face. The question was, was he the right person to provide it with these offspring.

Perhaps, Hans reasoned as he sat unmoving amidst the constant flux of the Hitler Youth surrounding him, he should approach a camp commandant and ask to be excused from this assignment. If he informed the Commandant that he had a young woman at home, to whom he wished to be faithful, there was a chance he would be sent back to Berlin. If the Commandant asked why he hadn't told his Leiter of his situation before he was transported, Hans could point to the tension of the imminent air raid, a certain confusion about the orders, and a last moment understanding with the girl with whom he wished to spend eternity.

Are you coming to dinner, Meitner? Willi's voice asked.

Hans shook his head. Willi shrugged indifferently and moved down the aisle with other Hitler Youth. Hungry as he was, Hans couldn't face the prospect of listening to his companions make obscene, anxious jokes about the task at hand. What was happening was far too serious for jokes. Even when, in his nightly fantasies, he subjected Frau Unger to a parade of increasingly bizarre indignities, there was nothing funny about it. Entering Frau Unger in her most private places was a sign of his contempt for her and all Jewesses. That he made her endure these indignities was as it should be, and would have been in real life had not all Jews been expelled from Berlin before they could fatally infect the Movement.

Hans waited til the last of the Cadre left, then, with a few others who had stayed behind, undressed and got into his pajamas. He found a towel Mutti had packed, along with a toiletries kit, and made his way to the communal bathroom, where he brushed his teeth, peed in a communal trough, glanced at the row of open, stainless steel toilets on the opposite wall, then turned and walked, barefoot, back to his cot. He slid in and shivered as his body absorbed the cold from the stiff sheet. Tired as he was, the cold bed felt bracing and, to his surprise, awakened memories of his previous night's visit to the Gibbler apartment, where, sitting thigh to thigh with Grussie, he felt her hand reach over, he thought to take his, but in fact to work its way up his thigh to his groin. The mere recollection of this gave him an erection. Her touch had been electric, and yet, at the same time had felt pure and generous, not at all like the sensations Frau Unger provided to him in his fantasies. What's more, her touch had felt tremendously surprising since up to that moment, Hans had exempted Grussie, both in thought and action, from sex. Can't someone make the lights go off? complained one of the Hitler Youth. The Fuhrer can, another Hitler Youth replied, but he's busy. The remaining boys, except for Hans, all laughed. Hans turned on his side and let his eyes drift shut. An image of Grussie swam up, smiling at him as she gripped his erect penis. Hans felt his breath congeal. He wanted to masturbate. Sleep seemed a million miles away. Yet, as he continued to lie on his side, sleep sped toward him. His thoughts became jumbled. He heard an inner voice speaking to him in language he couldn't understand. And just like that, he was asleep.

.2.

When he awakened, several hours later, to the sound of a bugle, it was to find that the world had turned completely white. The view outside was obscured by white coruscations on the insides of the naked windows and a milky light filtered into the dormitory, muting the faint glow of the electric lights which had come on again. Two SS stood in the doorway, delivering orders. They told the boys to shower, and then proceed to the dining hall which was located in the main building. Do you understand your orders, Youth? When the boys shouted their assent, the SS saluted, said Heil Hitler, and left.

Avoiding the general rush to the bathrooms, of which there were two, Hans made his bed and stowed the remainder of his gear in the small wardrobe provided to each Hitler Youth. The images from the day before were gone but their residue clung to him, making him feel slow and logy. Once his bed was made, Hans grabbed his towel, still damp from the night before, and made his way to the bathroom. The showers were already filled with dozens of naked adolescent bodies, all hairless and well formed, all tall, blond, and only recently through puberty. The oldest of the boys was seventeen. There were many sixteen year olds, a preponderance in fact, and a few fifteen year olds. The mood in the shower was one of strained jollity. The boys hid whatever anxieties they felt under a veneer of jokes and fellowship.

Hans hung his towel on a hanger and stepped into the showers. He turned on a shower head and stood a moment as the water warmed. A shower first thing in the morning was a luxury he hadn't enjoyed for more than two years. The absence of coal to fire the furnace, except at certain hours of the day, made this impossible. At Liebenswald apparently, there was no shortage of coal since some of the boys appeared, given their red skin, to have been under the hot water for some time now. Part of Hans rebelled against such excess, feeling that they should be conserving raw materials such as coal for the war effort; yet another part of him luxuriated in the warmth and was as reluctant as the other boys to leave it.

Impressive, Willi said suddenly, two shower heads over.

Hans blinked, then followed Willi's gaze to down his penis, with which Hans was too familiar to regard one way or the other. That someone would find it impressive both pleased and embarrassed him and made him turn red.

Look how shy she is, another boy said and a number of the Hitler Youth laughed. Never mind, Willi said to them. Look at yours and weep.

Hurry up Youth, a deep male voice commanded and the boys, sensing an SS, snapped to attention. Finish showering and proceed to the dining hall. Quickly!

Hans soaped himself, rinsed, and ran back to his bunk. Shivering, he dressed as quickly as possible, and was out the door in less than five minutes. All the buildings, the grounds, the surrounding forests, were clad in a deep mantle of fresh, weightless snow. The storm had ended but snow was still falling in flurries from the gray white sky. All sound appeared to have vanished.

Hans followed the other cadre to the main hall, his hair, like theirs, freezing as he ran. By the time he arrived, bits of ice clung to his hair. Once inside, Hans followed the mass of Hitler Youth down a short corridor into the dining hall which was large and airy, with high, unpainted ceilings, crossed by raw wooden beams that ran the width of the hall. Some fifty tables stood ready to receive them, covered in white table cloths with white dinner services gleaming at each place setting. At the rear of the dining hall, a conveyor ran along a serving area that was staffed by middle aged women dressed in white smocks and wearing hair nets. The women wore friendly, even motherly expressions, and asked each boy in turn if he wanted eggs, or oatmeal, or both, dishes that had become unheard of back home.

When his turn came, Hans asked for eggs. The serving woman, whose blue eyes sparkled in her ruddy, weathered face, asked Hans if he would like oatmeal as well, and Hans, unable to stop himself, said Yes so quickly the woman laughed, although good naturedly. Come back if you would like more, liebschen, she said as she passed him his food. Hans blinked, unused to being addressed so familiarly by an underling, never mind a stranger. But he nodded politely, accepted a cup of ersatz coffee and a glass of water from the next serving woman in the line, and made his way to a table where Willi was waving at him to join him.

Come. Come sit, Hercules, Willi said. The other boys looked away and guffawed.

Hans took a seat and began to eat, realizing as he devoured his oatmeal, that he hadn't eaten in an entire day and so, was ravenous. Again, he was engulfed by conversation in which he had no desire to participate. Talk revolved almost exclusively around girls. Hans wondered what it would have been like if they had been on a transport train to the eastern front, what they would said, whether their spirits would have been high or if each would have each sunk into the silence of his own thoughts and fears. The eastern front was, of course, the vital one. It was where the battle for the future of civilization was being waged. Either the Fuhrer would win, and the Russian beast would be pushed back into the red dirt from which it had emerged. Or, unthinkably, it would win, in which case it was better to die than to live under the savage, illiterate, Jew haunted regime that would pulverize them beneath its heel.

* * *

After breakfast, the boys were taken to the Liebenswald gymnasium for an hour of calisthenics, then told to shower once more and change into their dress uniforms. The second shower of the morning felt to Hans like a second meal. He couldn't believe this level of luxury existed in a country engaged in total war. It upset him, as though someone were consciously trying to make him soft.

Once they were dressed, Hans and the others from his Cadre stood in the barracks exchanging jokes and waiting. It seemed like hours before the doors opened and Dr. Shubert appeared with Dr. Franck and a high-ranking SS. The SS told the Cadres that they were to listen to Drs. Franck and Shubert as these latter two had information about the young women who had patriotically volunteered for Liebenswald with the aim of perpetuating the thousand year Reich. He concluded by saluting the two doctors and yielding his place to Dr. Shubert.

Dr. Shubert cleared his throat and opened by saying that no one would be forced to perform his duty since everything at Liebenswald was strictly voluntary. Nonetheless, he and his colleagues at the Institute For Genetic Purity had done extensive research on potential participants in their Experiment and on the basis of this research, had complete confidence in the ability of the Youth assembled before him to produce the healthiest and, in every conceivable respect, the most Germanic offspring possible. If, however, it should transpire that either party should find a pairing unsatisfactory, he was to report this fact to one of the Monitors and either Dr. Shubert himself, or Dr. Franck, would make all necessary adjustments.

During his talk, Hans was conscious of Willi making masturbatory gestures just out of view of the monitors. This infuriated Hans. It was bad enough they had to obey these orders without someone childishly mocking them. Childish mockery was the province of Jews and other degenerates, not of Hitler Youth, and especially, of Youth who were the children of aristocrats like Willi. At one point, Hans told Willi to stop and Willi complained that he hadn't come yet.

When Dr. Shubert finished, Dr. Franck accepted the megaphone and told the Cadres that selections had been made according to the most up to date scientific principles available. His own institute, the Institute For Aryan Reproduction, had employed cutting edge allele-based measurements to guarantee that the product of each individual collision of sperm and egg eventuated in the best possible genetic match. If any of the Hitler Youth had questions about their methodology, Dr. Franck or one of his associates would be happy to show him the specific chart the Institute had drawn up for him.

As Dr. Franck spoke, Willi unzipped his fly and seemed about to take out his penis when Hans, red in the face, hissed that if he did, he, Hans, would notify the SS. Willi, cool as always, shrugged and re-zipped his fly. Dr. Franck concluded by assuring the Cadres that the women knew what was expected of them and would do their part willingly and with the grace peculiar to German and Aryan women. Dr. Shubert seconded this with vigorous nod of his head and, after looking inquiringly at the two academics, the SS told the Cadres that males and females would meet for dinner and to wear their dress uniforms.

* * *

At six pm, after an afternoon spent watching films demonstrating sexual intercourse, reproduction, and childbirth, Hans and the rest of the Hitler Youth walked through the freezing cold to the dining hall, all wearing their dress uniforms, complete with medals and ribbons. Hans found himself between Willi and Karl Prusseldorf, the former whistling an American jazz tune, the latter half walking, half running to bat away the cold. When they reached the steps of the dining hall, Hans saw a second large complement of diners entering by the south entrance. He studied them a moment and realized these must be the women, or girls...the young women who, apparently, were now to be their dinner mates.

Once inside the refectory lobby, Hans and the other Hitler Youth stood a moment, shivering as their bodies shed cold and accustomed themselves to a rational temperature.

Feel your cock, Prusseldorf, Willi said. Make sure it hasn't gotten frostbite.

Prusseldorf and another H.J. Hans recognized as Martin Stuben, both put their hands under their pants. I can feel mine, said Prusseldorf.

I'm surprised, said Willi, I'm surprised you can feel it even when it's warm, Prusseldorf. Maybe what you're feeling is the absence of foreskin.

Shit head, muttered Prusseldorf as other H.J. laughed. A Leiter had appeared near the front of the massed boys and said something inaudible to those at the back.

What did he say? asked Stuben.

We're to sit four and four, four males four females, said another boy, not from their Cadre.

What if you're neither? asked Willi.

The mass of boys began to move, slowly at first, then gathering speed, toward the line of open French doors leading to the dining room. As he entered the vast space, Hans was aware that it smelled different. It smelled of toilet water and scented soap. Already arrayed at the tables, in groups of four, as far as the eye could see, were young women – Hans guessed their ages to be anywhere from seventeen to twenty five—all of them ruddy cheeked from the cold, well built, almost all blond with blue eyes. Their open faces, which seemed to have been cut from the same mold, were turned toward the doors with identical open, yet slightly startled, slightly embarrassed, slightly inquisitive expressions. At first, the effect of this mise en scene was to create a bottleneck, as Hitler Youth at the front of mass stopped at the entryways, uncertain what they were expected to do next. Seeing this, the Leiter, along with his assistants, began to shepherd those at the front toward tables at the rear of the dining hall, thus allowing the congestion behind them to slowly but steadily dissolve.

By the time it was Hans's turn to find a seat, the process had become methodical. Military even. Hitler Youth took the first available seat at the first available table. When that table was filled, they went to the next table. And the next. Hans took a seat not because he chose it, but because it was the next available. The farm girls were seated in every other chair insuring that the seating arrangement would be male, female, male, female, both around the table, and around the entire dining room. As long as the Hitler Youth continued to file into the dining hall, the psychic space between the boys and young women already seated was absorbed by the process. The noise of footsteps, the sound of chairs scraping as they were pulled back, of bodies lowering into seats, provided all the social interchange the two sexes felt necessary. The males and females would glance at one another, they couldn't help that, but then quickly turn their attention away from one another to the ritual of seat finding now being completed at the very front of the room. While it lasted, everyone appeared to find this variety of musical chairs extremely absorbing. However once it ended, a funereal silence settled over the immense hall, broken here and there by coughing.

Suddenly, Dr. Shubert appeared, out of nowhere as it seemed, and, standing on a small soapbox, began to address the assembled without the aid of a megaphone. Youth, Madchen, said Shubert, holding his hands together in front of his chest and rubbing them. Once again, welcome. You are here at last. This is a wonderful evening for me, for Reichfuhrer Himmler, for the Fuhrer, but, most of all, for Germany. There are moments in history which I admit may seem quite small when they are happening, but which, when one looks back at them, can be identified as turning points, pivots of the historical currents which flow from them. I believe this to be just such a moment.

Dr. Shubert smiled, and still kneading his hands, let his gaze wander to the ceiling. But enough of this, he said with a warm, if distant, smile. We are here tonight to get to know one another and, I hope, enjoy one another. After dinner, there will be mulled wine in the lobby while our dining hall is being cleared. There will then be a special treat!, a performance for you by the Liebenswald town orchestra, followed by a few moments to say Auf wiedersehn. Before you leave, you will each be given a copy of tomorrow's itinerary. The gods may yet make a contribution to tomorrow as it is supposed to snow. Gods, Dr. Shubert intoned, once more looking at the ceiling, behave yourselves!

At this, laughter swept the room. Dr. Shubert, sensing the moment was right, stepped down from his improvised dais and disappeared from view among the tall backs and shoulders of a group of leather clad SS, most of whom were in their fifties. Not knowing what else to do, the four hundred young men and women turned to one another and tiny conversations began to spring up about how funny Dr. Shubert was, how they hoped it would, or wouldn't, snow tomorrow, where they were from, how was the trip, was this their first visit to Liebenswald, wasn't it beautiful, did they like their rooms, where were they staying, and so forth. While the ice was being broken, waiters in white coats began to circulate through the room, each carrying several covered trays of food.

Hans sat erect in a middle chair between two young women, both with braids wound around the crowns of their heads. The young woman to Hans's left leaned over and said, It smells delicious, No? as a trolley of meals passed by. Hans nodded, his eyes locked on the far wall of the refectory. The young woman patted him on the forearm and told him not to worry. Hans reddened, but before he could reply she'd redirected her attention to Willi, who was sitting to her left. The young woman to Hans's right, who seemed shy, was answering questions put to her by Heinz Keltenfeuer, another member of Hans's cadre. Keltenfeuer asked her her name and she said Madchen.

That's not a name, Keltenfeuer said. It's a category. Just as Hans had, the girl, who could not have been more than eighteen, reddened. Looking at her plate, she murmured that, nonetheless, that was what her parents had named her. What was wrong with them? Keltenfeuer asked, apparently quite serious. Hans felt a sudden loathing for Keltenfeuer. He cleared his throat and asked Madchen where she was from. Hartz, she replied, so softly he had to strain to hear her. Have your people always lived in Hartz? Hans asked. Madchen nodded, staring at her place setting...a white napkin with tableware, the edge of the knife facing inwards. What do they do? asked Hans, placing his body so that Keltenfeuer, who was on the other side and three over from Madchen, could scarcely see her.

My father is a farmer, Madchen said, now beet red.

Ah, said Hans, what does he farm?

Dairy cows, said Machen, whose discomfort had reached a critical stage.

Don't mind Keltenfeuer, Hans said. He's an ass.

Madchen nodded without looking up.

He gives himself airs but his father is only a locksmith. His father joined the Party in '32 and Keltenfeuer thinks this makes his family aristocrats. He's number one hundred forty six in shooting, however, and one hundred forty overall, out of one hundred fifty Cadre.

What number are you? Madchen asked, again so softly Hans could barely hear her.

Five, Hans replied as a Waiter appeared and began placing their meals in front of them, lifting the cover only after the plate was securely on the table.

That's very high, Madchen said. Hans nodded, noting Madchen's fine, thin nose and the sprinkling of freckles faintly visible through the blush on each of her otherwise white cheeks.

What is your family name? Hans asked.

Kraus, said Madchen.

That's a good Aryan name, Hans said, lifting his knife and fork. Up to this point, he'd been scarcely conscious of the food. But the sudden aroma of meat now overwhelmed his senses and he realized he was extremely hungry. Not just hungry, famished, famished for the sort of meat, pork he guessed, which rested on his plate in a pool of light brown gravy. He cut into the meat and, forcing himself not to appear over anxious, raised it to his mouth. It was pork. His taste buds erupted into a spasm of ecstasy which, again, he managed to quash only by exercising all his considerable willpower. Had he been alone, Hans would have bolted the entire slice in a matter of seconds. Instead, he lay his knife and fork on the edge of the thick, white dinner plate, turned to Madchen and said, Eat. It's good.

Madchen again nodded, (she hadn't yet looked at him), and picked up her utensils. Hans waited until she had cut into her slice before returning to his own. This time, he ate more quickly. The entire dining room was now eating. Four hundred young men and women, long starved for pork, had suddenly fallen under its spell. Those who ate quickly finished their meat in a matter of seconds, and were left facing the small hill of mashed potatoes and gravy resting next to the still smaller hillock of canned peas. Those who ate their peas and potatoes first were reveling in the knowledge that the best part of the meal lay before them. A few, mostly males like Willi, had already consumed everything on their plate and were casting about for anyone who might be ill or nauseous or otherwise unable to finish their food. They were out of luck. Everyone guarded their plate with polite, but intense determination. Conversation appeared to have completely died out and, for a few moments, all Hans or anyone else could hear was the clink of tableware as it scraped against porcelain plates.

After he finished his meat, Hans took a drink of water. He had completely forgotten about the young women to either side of him. Leaning forward to spoon the last of his potatoes, he gazed past the first blond at Willi, who gazed back, wearing a mocking grin. Willi pointed at Hans's crotch and Hans glanced down, thinking he might have dropped food on his pants. When he looked up, Willi, ignoring him, was once more speaking to the voluble blond.

Would you like some of my pork? Hans heard someone say. The words were so unexpected that at first Hans thought he fantasized them. Madchen was gazing in his direction, not at him but at his plate. It was she who had offered him more pork.

No thank you, Hans said in a slightly strangled voice. You have it. I've had my share.

Madchen nodded, but cut off a small piece and placed it on Hans's plate. Hans exhaled. In their psychological warfare class, their professor had warned there might be times the enemy would attempt to extort information by establishing camaraderie. With enough training, the professor was confident, the Hitler Youth could be taught to endure, and resist, physical pain. It would be much harder at times to resist kindness.

In this case, however, Hans could think of nothing he needed to resist. So far as he could tell, Madchen was exactly what she appeared to be: a shy, eighteen year old farm girl with a generous heart. Had she been an enemy agent, those in charge of Liebenswald would have found her out. Instead what they had probably discovered was that she was of pure Aryan stock and therefore fit to conceive and raise the Aryan stock of the future.

Thank you, Hans said after a moment, staring at the piece of pork on his plate. Do you also raise pigs in your farm?

No, said Madchen. Just cattle. Which we don't eat. Unless they stop giving milk. We used to eat the ones that stopped giving milk, but no longer. Now they go the war effort.

Of course, said Hans. That's as it should be. He lifted his knife and addressed himself to the small slice of pork resting at the edge of the gravy. It was small enough that he could have bolted it at one go. But something told him to eat this piece more slowly.

We say a blessing before we slaughter them, Madchen continued, surprising Hans with her sudden talkativeness. Father says, Let us hope the meat the cow gives lightens the load of the poor boys who are fighting for us on the front lines.

Hans, his mouth full, felt suddenly guilty. He stole a look at Madchen to see whether she'd intended the irony of what she had just said. Her expression remained as open and free of nuance as ever. Still, the words stung. Not that Hans felt it was his fault he was at Liebenswald. He didn't want to be there. He wouldn't be, if he had anything to say about it.

Controlling himself, Hans swallowed the last mouthful of pork and began to eat the reconstituted mashed potatoes. Throughout the hall, conversation had resumed. Voices echoed off the cinderblock walls of the refectory, creating a stream of pleasant, almost musical noise which rose and fell as it absorbed individual sentences into its babbling current. Hans allowed the stream of noise to wash over him. It gave him a sense of immense well-being, almost as if he were home.

Are you still hungry? Madchen asked, almost inaudible in

the hum of conversation. Because I'm not going to have my potatoes.

Hans stared at her, unable to reply.

Potatoes make me too heavy, said Madchen, her hands folded in her lap. Later, maybe, when I'm pregnant, if I have to, I'll eat potatoes. She paused, then added, You have them.

Without waiting for an answer, Madchen lifted her plate and, in one smooth motion, slid the potatoes from her plate onto his. Hans shot a glance up the table, fearful that Willi had seen. But Willi, oblivious, was listening earnestly to his blond.

You shouldn't do this, Hans said. You need strength too.

Madchen was silent for a moment, before replying, I'm as strong as a horse.

Hans laughed, the first genuine laugh he could remember having since the carpet bombing began. If you're as strong as a horse, what does that make me? he said when he'd caught his breath.

But you're a man, said Madchen, her eyes averted. Men are always stronger than women. German men especially.

* * *

What do you think..., Dr. Shubert asked, scraping out the bowl of his favorite meerschaum pipe, What do you think your Grussie would say about our mission? It was now an hour after dinner and Hans and Dr. Shubert were seated in Shubert's private office, the office in which, when Shubert wasn't coun-seling troubled youth, he conducted official correspondence, pondered important policy questions, and, occasionally, read from a private library the SS had confiscated from a collector and bestowed as a gift on the camp administrators.

She, Hans began, but then stopped. Up to now, his internal debates on the question had taken a negative response on Grussie's part for granted. But the way this scrunched up, over-weight, faintly Jewish looking doctor framed the question had given him pause. After all, Grussie was not simply a girl, but a German girl. Could a German, even a woman, reasonably object to policies meant to advance the well-being of all Germans? For the first time since he began to probe this question, Hans felt uncertain. He glanced at Shubert, who continued to scrape away at his pipe, then past Shubert and out the window, where snow had once more begun to fall. She would be hurt, Hans said at length, feeling this was the correct answer.

Yes, of course, said Dr. Shubert, proceeding to the stage he loved most: loading the pipe with fresh tobacco and tamping it down with the small silver tamp his wife had given him for their thirtieth anniversary. After all, he continued, still thinking of Gertl, his wife, women navigate by emotion. The poor things are made that way. The news that her beloved has fathered a child by another woman would naturally cause your Grussie pain. But let us suppose, you and I, that we put it to Grussie whether she supports Lebensborn. What would the young lady say?

She would say, Hans frowned, feeling he was being tied in knots, She would say we must do whatever is necessary for the Fuhrer to complete his vision.

Now suppose the Furher, and Reichfuhrer Himmler, felt that it was necessary for you to participate in Lebensborn; what would Grussie say to this? Here Shubert, not expecting an answer and not receiving one, lit his pipe and exhaled the first load of pale gray blue smoke into the square, low ceilinged room, furnished, by Gertl, with antiques and furniture from a local Jewish household.

She would say, Dr. Shubert answered his own question, that you must do as you are ordered, even if what you are ordered to do causes me pain. This is what any good German female would say. This, in fact, is what the wives and mothers of men we send to the front say. Take our Karls and Jurgens and Hanses, even if it means we will never see them again. Sanctify, if you must, our holy cause with our children's' blood. Is this not so? Or am I exaggerating?

Instead of answering immediately, Hans allowed himself a moment to imagine the pleasure it would give him to lift the bust of Beethoven sitting on Doctor Shubert's desk and brain him with it. This lasted but a second, before Hans's innate sense of order reasserted itself. I understand what you are saying Herr Doctor, Hans replied, and I am completely willing to die for the Reich. But there is a difference between dying for the Reich and...

Copulating for it? Dr Shubert interjected as Hans paused.

Hans said nothing. For a moment, neither did Dr Shubert. The two sat absorbing the heat from the low fire flickering in Dr. Shubert's fireplace. The flames licked up and around a newly positioned log, then withdrew to the logs beneath and smoldered there for a time before staging a fresh assault on the fresh wood. Hans watched, fascinated. Dr. Shubert let his eye follow Hans's and for a while, he too stared at the battle being fought between the fire and wood. It was unclear which would win. The fire retreated to gain support from the coals which burned underneath it, but this allowed the log to cool and gather its resources for the next attack. Who won would depend on how much energy was left in the coals, how green the wood was, the specific density of the wood, the temperature of the fire, drafts, weak points in the bark, and so on. It would be impossible to know from watching these early engagements how the battle would end. He would have to wait and see.

.3.

Feeling that a change had come over the room, Hans sat a few moments in silence. Dr Shubert showed no inclination to break the silence. Finally Hans roused himself. To breed a man and a woman, he said, is no different from breeding a stallion and mare. The only difference is in the feeling the man has for the woman.

Dr. Shubert slumped lower in his chair, tented his fingers, and seemed to consider this. Yes, he said. You are right. That is why, my friend, when we want a race horse, we breed a stallion who has won races with a mare who has won races. You would not breed a stallion with a mule, or a mule with a stallion, if you wanted to win races, no? That would make no sense.

Not all horses can win a race, Hans said. Only one can.

Not all have to, said Dr. Shubert, speaking very softly. It is only important that all the horses in the race can run quickly and therefore might win. That is what we try to assure here. Not that every child will grow up to be a Fuhrer. But that any one of them might. All will be Aryans, of the purest blood line. That is as much as we can do.

The child Grussie and I will have will be a pure Aryan, Hans countered.

Yes. If you come back from the war. Or…if she agrees to have a baby with you before you leave.

The more Dr. Shubert slumped in his chair, the straighter Hans sat. Yet he no longer felt angry or defensive. The problem posed by Dr. Shubert interested him. He wanted to solve it.

There is no guarantee I will father a child here either, he said.

Are you afraid you won't be able to? asked Dr. Shubert.

Of course not, Hans said, flaring. That is not it.

Shubert nodded, tamped his pipe into a huge ashtray and once again began to clean it, nodding all the while. Yes, he said, You are what gives me the most satisfaction. Youth such as yourself, who come here doubting us, express your doubts, and force us to justify our purposes. When I tell the Reichfuhrer about you, he often laughs with pleasure. The others, the ones who come and do their duty and go home boasting about it, well, they too are wonderful, wonderful Aryan boys, but just boys. Their children will look like gods. But yours, well, my young friend...

Shubert, now sitting almost perpendicular to the chair seat, his stomach rising in front of his chest, sighed. Do you think any of our soldiers, our millions of brave soldiers, could participate in Lebensborn No. That would not be the case. Pure as they are, most of them, our project can accept only the best. You see, all of us, any one of us, can die for the Fuhrer, but only the best of us can reproduce for him. That is why you are here, and not at home with Grussie. Grussie may well be the best of all possible mates for you, even the best. But we cannot know that. Whereas, with the young women we've assembled here, we are certain of them. Have you met one yet?

Hans stiffened, then nodded.

What is her name? asked Dr. Shubert.

Madchen. Madchen Kraus, said Hans.

A good Aryan name, said Dr. Shubert. Do you like her?

Hans, rigid, nodded a second time.

Good. Don't feel guilty, Shubert said, struggling to his feet. Do what your German soul tells you. And if you need to talk again, this is what I am here for.

* * *

As he finished snapping on his galoshes and buttoning his overcoat, Dr. Shubert reviewed the conversation he'd just conducted with the Hitler Youth. In a sense, the problem posed by the young man was temporal. There was simply no longer enough time. They had to make do with what they had and make do with it immediately. Who knew what lay in store for Germany, and thus, for this, the most profound of experiments.

Dr. Shubert checked his pockets for his reading glasses, turned out the lights, then turned them on again as he remembered his pipe. He placed the pipe in the free pocket of his topcoat, extinguished the lights once and for all and walked out of the office into the small waiting room. Bounce light from the snow illuminated the waiting area and Dr. Shubert walked purposefully to the front door, and out into a curtain of flurries. The last strains of the great Ride Of The Valkerie wafted up into the night from the Assembly hall and caused him to pause a moment to hum along. What power, what unearthly power was contained in those chords. What vision and power and majesty. Cold began to seep into his galoshes and Dr. Shubert resumed walking. Gertl would be waiting for him. No matter how late he returned from his duties, she would be sitting up, often after the fire had gone out, knitting, or reading, or sometimes, merely rocking in her rocking chair. She needed to assure herself he was safe before she could sleep. The thought made Dr. Shubert smile. Thirty one years of marriage and she still took care of him as if they were newlyweds. Thirty one years.

In the early days of the program, when there was still all the time in the world, things had been entirely different. There was no need to legislate events. You merely had to put young SS together with fertile young women and things would take their course. True, some of the SS had been married. But there were so many candidates then for Lebensborn, and so much latitude, that they could do what they wished without judgment or supervision. The assumptions then were general, not specific as they were now. A certain number of fruitful copulations would result in a certain number of births. Multiply these by the thousand years they were confident would be given them and the net would be hundreds of thousands, even millions of perfectly formed, exquisitely fine- tuned ubermensch. Why hurry, why push, when you strode alongside Destiny. Why not lie back, lie back and let the wave carry you?

All this, Dr. Shubert thought to himself as he trod through the dry, lightly packed snow, was over now. Now, to produce even a few hundred more ubermensch was a race against time. There had even been those who favored scrubbing the program entirely, arguing it was a luxury the Reich could no longer afford. He had been present, Dr. Shubert recalled, at Wannsee when they made this argument to Himmler himself in the great Hall Of The Gods. Himmler sat at the head of the Lion's Table, impassive but alert as, one by one, Generals stood to paint the grimmest of pictures and enunciate the direst of needs. They would need everyone they could lay their hands on. They would need men over sixty, and boys over fourteen. Lebensborn was all very well and good when the troops could take a vacation. Now, it was merely a distraction.

Himmler had heard them out, then turned to him, to Dr. Martin Shubert, and asked, What do you think?

This was the first time in two years the Reichfuhrer had addressed him directly.

Dr Shubert had cleared his throat, and looking only at the Reichfuhrer, had said that Lebensborn was not a distraction, but the seedbed of everything they were trying to accomplish. Without Lebensborn, without the marriage it represented of Science and Destiny, the entire experiment, the overthrow of a weak and corrupt government, the conquest of Belgium and France, the purging of undesirable elements, was incomplete, if not meaningless. It was only by replacing weakness with strength, imperfection with beauty, subversion with purpose that they could justify the work and pain and blood that had gone into the Experiment. To abandon Lebensborn now, because it was difficult to sustain, would be to abandon the entire underpinnings of their ideology.

Himmler had listened to this impassively, then asked the Generals if they would accept a Lebensborn where Hitler Youth were assigned to the program and required to complete their work within a set period of days, four at most. The Generals had looked at one another, then Jodl rose and said this would be acceptable, unless circumstances changed dramatically for the worse. They had come, Dr Shubert said to himself, holding his gloved thumb and forefinger a centimeter apart, this close to losing the entire program. Only his passion, his vision, his!, had saved it. Yet even this had come at a price. Young Hans would be paired with young... Dr Shubert had forgotten her name. He would be asked, in theory, but ordered, in practice, to mate with the young woman and, what's more, to do so on a strict timetable. No longer was the natural law of attraction to be a defining element of the Experiment. Doctors and geneticists would dictate who would pair with whom.

As he came even with the Great Hall, all of whose windows were illuminated, Dr. Shubert paused for a second time and peered in. Many of the windows were frosted over, some from the outside, some from condensate produced by the steady breathing of hundreds of healthy young bodies. The contrast between the whiteness of the Great Hall's walls and the warm yellow of its many windows gave the building a surreal, almost insubstantial look, as if it were not a huge wooden structure but rather, a vast painting. This sense was reinforced by the unearthly quiet of the night, the damped silence of the snowed over fields, the arcs of white light cast onto the snow by the sodium lamps. This far from the cities, there was no need for them to worry about light. No one would come to bomb them. No one knew they were here. They were, for all the enemy knew, a tiny village at the edge of a great forest.

Dr. Shubert shivered and resumed walking. What, he wondered as he turned up his collar and pulled his scarf tighter around his neck, brought this on? That's right. The young man. The youth's qualms that, by copulating with…what was her name?… he would be betraying his young woman, his beloved. Dr. Shubert nodded. Yes, the human tragedy was not always acted out on a grand scale. At times, it was confined to the tiny stage of a single naive individual. Dr. Shubert felt he had convinced the boy that it was his duty as a citizen, as a member of the Hitler Youth, to couple with the girl. And after all, Dr. Shubert smiled to himself as a sudden gust of wind blew snow into his face, there were worse fates. The boy would probably encounter one. And yet, there was something in all this that gnawed at him, something he couldn't deny. It was that, in the end, the boy was right. In order to produce an ideal, you had to work from an inner ideal. You couldn't compel an ideal from the outside. You could clean from the outside. You could rid the body of undesirable elements. You could ensure that imperfections, physical and psychological, were ruled out of the genetic equation. You could triage the best of the best. But no matter how hard you tried, you couldn't probe your way into the soul of another human being and tinker with its most basic constituents. These you had to assume as first principles.

In most cases, this limitation posed no difficulty. The boys came willingly these days, shyly, true, but willingly. They were embarked on a great adventure, not just the perpetuation of the Reich, but initiation into the mystery of themselves as sexual beings. It was only when someone like young Hans, someone who invoked love in opposition to duty, that the potential costs of this process rose to the surface and became manifest.

Well, Dr. Shubert said to himself as behind him the doors of the Great Hall opened and Youth began to pour back out into the black and white night, So be it.

III

.1.

To say the knock on the door was unexpected was a great understatement. Dr. Shubert was tempted to ignore it as an accident but it sounded again, accompanied by Dr. Franck's urgent appeal that he open up. Dr. Shubert said he would be there in a moment, withdrew his penis from his wife's upraised bottom, and rushed to the bathroom. He washed his member, put on a dressing gown, composed himself, and strode, flushed but outwardly collected, to the front door. It was snowing heavily and snow fell off Franck's shoulders and shoes as he and the SS Dr. Shubert recognized as the camp Sturmbahnfurher entered without further explanation.

I'm sorry to interrupt you, Herr Doktor, the Sturmbahnfuhrer, Erhard Lenz, apologized, but it's quite urgent.

We are facing a crisis, Franck said, his ashen face underlining his words.

I have just learned, Lenz continued as if Franck hadn't spoken, that the Russians have broken through near Poznan. While there's been no determination at the moment of what course we will take, all available troops are to report to their assembly points by five tomorrow evening. This includes Hitler Youth age fifteen and over.

Ah, said Dr. Shubert with a sinking feeling as his wife padded into the room, rubicund and grandmotherly as always, her woolen bathrobe and reindeer faced slippers giving the lie to what they had just been doing. Would anyone like coffee? she asked, rubbing her hands together and peering nearsightedly, but with a smile, at the two men.

No...Yes, said Dr. Shubert. Yes, Gertl. Make us coffee please.

Gertl disappeared into the interior of the house and Shubert once again faced his two visitors.

I've contacted the Reichfuhrer, said Franck...

We too were in contact with Reichfuhrer Himmler, said Lenz, preempting Franck. There was a temporary delay getting through, understandable under the circumstances, but when the Reichfuhrer called back, he said our work here merited a stay of several hours and could we please complete it by morning so as to have the Hitler Youth on the next available train to their home base. We of course said Yes, that would be possible.

I see, said Dr. Shubert. So we must push things up to... tonight.

I've already, Franck began...

This is correct, said Lenz. I have informed the housekeeping staff to prepare cabins for immediate occupancy and asked the entertainment staff to keep the Youth at the symphonic hall until we are able to address them.

Let me put on my clothes right away, said Dr. Shubert, grasping the grave nature of the situation immediately and wasting no time responding to it. Coffee of course would now have to wait. Everything would. The contingency he had just been handed threw the success of the entire experiment into question. Studies had shown that the fertilization rate among Youth increased in direct proportion to the time they were given to adapt--which, interestingly enough, was in marked contrast to earlier periods of the Experiment when it was found couplings were most productive on night ONE of the SS arrival at Liebenswald, dropping off thereafter in both the frequency of congresses and their outcome.

Why this should have been, Dr. Shubert mused as he wrestled himself back into his long underwear, was a mystery. But it was undeniable. With each passing day the SS tended to have more to do with one another and less with the young women brought there to mate with them. Though mate was not the right word. Perhaps the SS's withdrawal was due to a sexual anxiety which, while it could be suppressed in the first flush of female companionship, reasserted itself once the male's immediate needs had been satisfied. The SS, as Dr. Shubert well knew, were charged with immense and often disturbing tasks. Most of them suffered these silently, which was itself problematic, as the severe workload and relentless pace to which they were subjected couldn't help but generate significant psychic pressure. No one would argue that these tasks shouldn't be executed as quickly as possible, yet neither would anyone deny that such haste, necessary as it was, took an inevitable toll.

Dr. Franck and Standartfuhrer Lenz were sipping coffee when Shubert returned, but on his arrival, quickly drained their cups and stood. After declining a coffee of his own, Dr. Shubert gave Gertl a chaste kiss goodbye and followed the others into the swirling snow. Lenz led the way. Franck coming second and Dr. Shubert, head down, bringing up the rear. The expression, bringing up the rear, reminded Shubert of the sexual intercourse the arrival of Lenz and Franck had interrupted. In truth, his and Gertl's sex life should have ended long ago. And in fact, had ended prior to his transfer to Lebensborn. Not that he didn't still love Gertl. Nor was he put off by her somewhat altered body, an inevitability in a woman who had borne four children. No. It was rather than the domestic turn necessitated by the children's arrival, combined with the intense work load he undertook as hostilities progressed, had eaten into their joint libido. They would still have intercourse on their anniversary, July 15th. But for the rest of the year, their sex life remained something each of them did or didn't recall in private.

With the advent of Lebensborn, all this changed. One evening Dr. Shubert happened to mention to Gertl what they were actually doing at Liebenswald and her interest was keen enough that he quickly found himself describing in detail the protocols that had been drawn up to ensure young German women were assigned to appropriate SS partners. Surprisingly, Gertl went on to manifest an equally keen interest in the mechanics of the sexual contact, where it occurred, how the young women felt about it, whether there were failures of nerve, and so forth. This talk, to both their surprise, led them in short order to bed, where they had their first passionate engagement of the past twenty years.

Nor did things stop there. Each began to look forward to those evenings when Dr. Shubert would return home early and regale Gertl with tales of the day's activities--what the SS looked like, what the madchen looked like, what Himmler wanted from the program, rumors about the Fuhrer's sexual proclivities, (which both found especially stimulating), where sex took place, and how often. Dr. Shubert, who, like his wife, had put on a few pounds, began to find in his and her corpulence, an incentive to ever more creative and arcane couplings. A result of this sexual activity was that the two began to lose weight, though neither mentioned it to the other for fear it might cause them to retreat from positions, methods, and language which they had begun to find erotically necessary.

The entertainment hall floated into sight, looming out of the snow as a blurry ball of light. Rubbing his eyes, Dr. Shubert followed Franck into the warm interior. For a moment, he felt nothing as he stamped his feet and clapped his gloved hands Lenz was saying something unintelligible, and it was only when Dr. Shubert remembered he was wearing earmuffs that he felt he hadn't gone deaf from the cold.

...to address them, he heard Lenz declare as his hearing returned. It goes without saying we do not want to give out privileged information. So you will merely say that transportation issues have decreed the Hitler Youth's imminent return to their staging points which has in turnnecessitated an acceleration of the week's schedule. Then you, Dr Franck, will read out the room assignments alphabetically and chronologically. While waiting for rooms to become available, the Youth will be encouraged to socialize in the entertainment hall, either with one another or with their intended partner.

Dr. Shubert stopped listening. Feeling had returned to his fingers and toes and, with it, the surreal sense that this might be the last session of Lebensborn over which he would ever preside. The Russians were in Poznan. Could they be stopped? Dr. Shubert doubted it. Much as he wanted to believe in the Fuhrer and the will of the German, in his heart of hearts he believed that the brutality and savagery of this particular unter-mensch, along with the sheer volume of it, would eventually carry the day. That this would be a social and cultural tragedy went without saying. But it would also be, and for him this was far, far more important, a biological tragedy. What they had tried to achieve with Lebensborn was nothing less that the trans-formation of the human species. Yes, the first step toward that goal had involved cleansing the population of undesirable and retrograde elements...retards, mutants, and the like. And the second, bold and visionary step, had been, and continued to be, to remove the Jew. Regarded scientifically, however, these were negative, even regressive steps. They removed elements that shouldn't have been there in the first place. Whereas Lebens-born was a positive step in that it attempted to supplement and finally replace a compromised genetic present with a transcendent future. The brilliantly simple idea that you could do with human beings what you did with livestock had, when he first learned of it, taken Dr. Shubert's breath away. Of course. Of course. The beautiful thing did not have to come about by chance. It could be managed. Man made.

Now that he was warm enough to move about, Dr. Shubert removed his topcoat, scarf, and hat, and, handing them to an SS subaltern, made his way to the front of the entertainment hall, where the thousand Hitler Youth and young women gazed up at him expectantly. He could almost feel their attention as something palpable, a force field that gripped and held him in place as surely as if it were a gigantic magnet. He could work with this field. He must work with it.

Youth, he began. Forgive us for keeping you up past your bedtime.

Everyone laughed. Even Lenz, who was standing to one side fooling with his affected monocle, permitted himself a small smile.

The reasons for this are totally out of our control. As you know, man these days is subject to machine, and machine, in the form of our great German railway system, has informed us that our Hitler Youth must, must, you understand, be transported to their home locations no later than tomorrow morning.

Here and here a few groans gave way to a silence that was almost audible.

Don't ask your Dr. Shubert why. He is as much in the dark about this as you are. What I do have to tell you, however, I am not in the dark about. It is this: we have tonight and tonight only to complete the great task for which we have come together.

Taking a deep breath, Dr. Shubert poured a glass from the water jug that sat just inside his lectern. He was very thirsty and drained its entire contents before continuing. I understand this may perhaps make some of you anxious. This I assure you is completely normal. You are the best we have, but even you are not superhuman. Here Dr. Shubert paused, drank from a freshly filled glass, then added, Not yet anyway.

Laughter erupted throughout the great hall and Dr. Shubert smiled. When I am finished speaking, you will receive your room assignments and then, those of you for whom there is time, will repair to those rooms to become intimate with one another. Let us not speak in euphemisms here. Our desire is that you produce what we, and the Reichfuhrer, and our glorious Fuhrer, and our glorious Reich, awant and need more than anything else at this critical moment in our history. And since there is as yet only one known way to produce this...

Again, the room exploded in laughter, some of it, the boys', high pitched, others, the young women's, softer and more knowing. Since there is only one way of producing this, Dr. Shubert repeated, that is the path which we would like you to take. You are the best and the healthiest and most principled and most visionary and the truest and purest we have. You may go to your little rooms afraid, afraid that you cannot do what we ask, or that what comes from your doing it will not live up to our expectations, that you are doing something wrong, or the wrong thing. But you should know, Youth and Madchen, that when you enter these rooms, our glorious Reich goes with you. And not only our Reich, but the spirit and heart of the Reichfuhrer. And not only of the Reichfuhrer. Here Shubert lowered his voice and again sipped from his glass...but of the Fuhrer himself. The spirit of our national soul, our blood, goes with you. Our Leader and Father goes with you.

The room, with its thousand occupants, was so quiet you could have heard, except for the sighing of the wind and the pitter patter of snow against the windows, a pin drop. Dr. Shubert, who knew he had a tendency to find an oratorical thread and ride it until it became tired and slack, this time understood that his speech was over--that, no matter how much he wanted to continue, this was the proper place to stop. Rather than stopping right away, however, he lifted his now half full glass, and, in the continuing silence of the hall, drank it to the end. Then he raised his arm in salute, and quietly, feelingly, with all the emotion he had ever felt for the great Experiment which was now coming to an end, said Heil Hitler.

A moment later, a thousand voices responded with a unitary, deafening, Heil Hitler of their own. And Dr. Shubert, his head and shoulders bowed, left the lectern and disappeared into the darkened wings of the great hall.

Bundestag. Reichhalle. Hall of Heroes, Nuremberg Stadium. Leibenswald. Wolf's Lair. Eagle's Nest. 1131 Vielenstrasse, Apartment 505. No. Apartment 408. Four hundred eight. Apartment four hundred eight from apartment five hundred five is Apartment 103, one hundred three. Who lives in Apartment 103? The neighbor is in 303. A palindrome. We studied the palindrome in Numerology. Numerology, which only corrupt Jewish dogs consider nonsense. Numerology is the key to Life. One hundred three. One hundred three.

Hans rubbed his eyes. One hundred three. One hundred three is across from the mail boxes but is not the Super. The Super is in the basement. Apartment 1. One hundred three...A prime number.

He'd never been in three hundred three, where his mother conducted her affair with the neighbor. Rolph, Hans remembered, cheeks burning. You see Madchen, my mother fucks our neighbor. This is why my cheeks are red. Because my mother, who is married to my father, who may be dead, has sexual intercourse with a neighbor. Is 303 a Prime? No. 101 goes into three oh three three times. Three times one is 3, three times 0, three times three once more. You see? Easy. What about 101? Is this a Prime?

It's still snowing? What's taking them so long? How long does it take to remove your clothes and ejaculate? Twenty minutes, according to Willi Von Stauffenberg. There are nineteen letters in his name. A Prime Number. Take it off, put it in, take it out, put it on. Twenty minutes at most. Ten minutes to change the sheets, clean the bathroom. That makes thirty.

Why so quiet, Madchen? Even cows moo. They should give us schnapps. If we are old enough to fuck, we are old enough to drink. Frau Brest lives in 603. She is the conscience of the building. What building? I told you. 1131 Vielenstrasse. A good,, Jew-free Berlin building. Six stories. Twenty four apartments. Twenty three, plus the Super's. We used to be four in three rooms. Now we are three in five rooms. They pulled the Jewess out by the hair. She howled like...like...

No. She emerged holding her daughter's hand. Tall Jew

daughter. Tall among dwarves. Mutti. If they hadn't come, they wouldn't have needed to go. What is under that skirt? Another skirt. And under that? Wool stockings? And under that. What is under the wool stockings? First the coat. Then the jacket. Then the skirt. Then the underskirt. The slip. Then the wool stockings. Green wool stockings. Then the leg flesh. Thigh flesh. Ripe, full quivering, /warmcold thigh flesh. Then what? Six steps. Coat. Jacket. Skirt. Underskirt. Stockings. Underpants. Silk underpants? Underpants. Pull down the underpants. Six steps. Spread the legs. Try not to look. Look above it. At the blond hair. It is blond, isn't it?

Ach. You startled me, Herr Doktor. Yes, I enjoyed speaking with you too, Herr Doktor. Yes. I have decided. Madchen. No, that is her name. She comes from a farm. Schwabia. No no. Hartz. We live in a vacant apartment. Via the Jews. We fumigated it. Some China, a couch. We previously owned our own furniture, you see. We carried it downstairs. The Super helped. Karl, our Super. Very strong. An ox. But lame. A lame ox. (Laughter). Lots of wood, dark wood molding. Around the doors too. I don't know its name. Lintel? The lintel too. Dark wood. Windows with mullions. White and gray walls. Some scratches because the movers...Thank you. You too, Herr Doktor. Heil Hitler.

No one. Dr. Shubert. I thought so too. His nose however is too small. Intelligensia are physically small. Their brains need more blood. Like Jew noses. So much blood goes to the nose, the prick suffers. This is why Jews are circumcised: to free blood for the nose. You laugh, but this is science. Prime numbers and circumcision: branches of science. Meitner. Two "e's." The first "e" goes to Market. Why are you laughing? What are you wearing under your skirt? No, and yes.

Yes, I have never done it. No, I have done it dozens of times. Frau Unger. I bend her over her bed. No no no. Three hundred six. Five rooms. Carved moldings. Bay windows. Wood floors... what is it called? Yes, herringbone. Like my penis. Herring bone. First a limp herring. Then a bone. Where was I? In Frau Unger. Let me tell you, Madchen...Is it hot in here? Or is it me? I would... First I would write orders. Be ready at 7. Maybe I will come then. Maybe later. Maybe I will come at three in the morning. I knock loud, like...I want to find your dress up, over your fat waist.

Underpants around your fat knees. Legs spread. That big black
Jewish forest facing front. Udders hanging out. Now, please to
turn around Frau Unger and place your hands on the mattress.
Face me with your buttocks. Big white pillows. You are crying?
You will wake the children.
        Reich Halle. Bundestag. Wolf's Lair. Eagle's Nest. Ten letters.
Nine letters. Nine letters. Ten letters.
        Hans Meitner. Eleven letters.
        Madchen Kraus. Eleven letters.
        Adolph Hitler. Twelve letters.

.3.

Next morning, the train was already idling at the platform, white smoke pulsing from its engine, as trucks arrived bearing the Hitler Youth. Sicherdienst ushered the Youth out of the unheated trucks, through snow, into the warm train cars, making it plain there was no time to lose. Snow, falling since yesterday, would provide temporary cover, but it would be hours before they reached home. Anything could happen. The weather could turn. The sun could come out. They would be sitting ducks.

Hans stumbled down the wet aisle until a Sicherdienst shoved him into a compartment. He could barely keep his eyes open. He dropped into a seat, as it happened, situated between Prusseldorf and Kline and immediately fell asleep. Someone stepped on his foot, Rafe Vaterboren, and Hans woke. Exhaustion hung on him like a blanket. Prusseldorf said he was taking up too much room. Hans ignored him. Willi reached past Hans and cuffed Prusseldorf's ear.

Just because you couldn't get it up, he said, that is no reason to abuse others.

I got it up, Prusseldorf protested.

This is not what I heard, said Willi, cuffing him again.

The other boys laughed. Hans was aware of the engine vibrating through the compartment floor. It was giving him yet another erection. He pulled his coat tight and tried to go back to sleep. A whiff of Madchen's perfume hid in the coat. He remembered what her vagina looked like and blinked in surprise. Then put it out of his mind. In six hours, he would be home. There, he could sleep uninterrupted.

...Meitner here, Hans heard Willi saying, got off three salvos for Deutschland. Each a direct hit. I have it on good authority that Reichfuhrer Himmler himself plans to give Meitner the highest possible honor, Prick Of The Third Reich...

Shut up, Von Stauffenberg, Kline said. You'll get yourself shot.

Willi tapped Hans on his knit cap. Don't listen to them, Meitner, he said. They're jealous. Those of them who had the chance to fuck spent it saying This has never happened to me before.

Kline tried to punch Willi but couldn't extricate his arm from Prusseldorf's side. Willi lit a cigarette, then offered the pack to Hans, who took one. Hans felt too tired to smoke and too tired not to. It would help him sleep. Her thing, swollen when he examined it, was pale pink on the outside, the inner lips clearly defined as if they had been outlined in pen. Atop and to the sides were dustings of blond hair, short, faintly stiff, but soft too, like drying wool. He hadn't wanted to look but couldn't help himself. Madchen had let him. She asked if he'd like her to open it and he'd shaken his head No. This was afterwards. After he had put it in and come. She was lying on her back with her legs in the air to help his sperm find her egg. She said she knew it would because a woman can tell when she'd been impregnated. They would make an Aryan child for the Reich. As Hans looked at her vagina, she asked what he'd like to name it. When he didn't answer, she said, It depends. Is it a boy or a girl? If it is a girl, we will name it Heide, after my mother. What should we name the boy?

Hans tore his gaze away from the swollen pink lips and looked at Madchen. Her face was flushed. They were lying, he was sitting actually, on a single bed in a small, whitewashed room, heated by a single electric coil. Snow brushed the windows, which were covered in pale cotton curtains. A solitary lamp with a parchment shade lit the room. Now and then, the wind rose and the entire room would shake.

Two more minutes, Madchen said. She had helped him get in. At first, he didn't become erect but she helped with that too. She took it between her hands and talked to it, then put it in her mouth and hummed. Hans almost died. He felt he'd almost died. In reality, he grew hard immediately and she took it out saying how big it was. She rolled him onto her and aimed it and helped him ease it in. It went in easily. It felt like it got even bigger in there. She was saying something. He wasn't certain what. Fuck me, liebschen, he thought, but that couldn't be it. He didn't remember. He came very quickly. Exploded was more like it. He moved and exploded into her, releasing a tremendous pressure. He felt it climb up him and explode. Then he lay there as she stroked his back and cooed at him. Sang to him. A farm song, maybe.

The train jerked, moved forward a few feet, then stopped.

71

Willi was still talking. He was saying something about the Front. How, in a matter of days, they would be at the front and idiots like Prusseldorf would die virgins, which was good because the last thing in the world Germany needed was little Prusseldorfs. What Germany needed, Hans knew, feeling his erection bounce against his pants, was little Hans/Madchens. He had wanted to fuck her again, but she insisted he roll off so she could put her legs in the air. He said he would take longer this time but she smiled and said he had done fine, wonderfully, and now was the time for her to do her job. For the Reichfuhrer, and the Fuhrer. And the Reich. It would not do to waste his good work by not doing hers.

One minute, she'd said, when there were footsteps in the hall. Someone knocked on their door and said, Ten minutes. One minute. Ten minutes. Nine minutes wouldn't be time for them to do it again. They had to dress, put on their winter coats, wash their hands and...then meet in the hallway where they would be escorted to...wherever they would be escorted to.. Hans put his hand under a breast and lifted it. It felt heavy, dead weight, but supple, alive. The nipple was raised and he put his head down and kissed it, took it in his mouth, sucked it. It tasted humid, like...like nothing he'd tasted before. There was a tiny bit of blond hair under her raised arms. Her feet were against the wall, that was it. He kissed her open mouth and slid his tongue in, finding her tongue. She moved her tongue against his, two tongues, slithering against each other. Again he felt himself getting hard. Perhaps there would be time. But the voices in the hall sounded just outside; they would hear them. No time, Madchen said as she lowered her legs. He lifted a leg and kissed the inside of the thigh, the thick muscle quivering under white skin. Goosebumps. She reached down and pushed her fingers through his hair. Could he kiss it? He wasn't sure. It might harm the baby. He didn't know.

The train jerked a second time and began to glide along the tracks. Hans heard more laughter but not what caused it. The laughter died away, replaced by the repetitive sound of the iron wheels. Ba dum, ba dum, ba dum, ba dum. He was no longer a virgin. Hans Meitner. A man at fifteen. A father. Hans grinned, not certain if he was awake or asleep. What would Frau Unger say, as he bounced her tits from side to side, slapped them from side to side, his teeth gritted as he pounded away. I'm a Father, Jew, he'd inform her. A German parent. He would lean his weight on her back and pull on her tits. That would show the Jewess. Jewess. The word felt like chewed meat in his mouth. Jewess.

He was falling asleep. He was asleep. He was home. At the Station. Mutti and Heike were waiting for him, bundled up against the wind that blew down the platform. Mutti looked anxious. Heike was holding a flag at her side, swinging it back and forth like a purse. Mutti uttered a cry when she saw him and raced forward, embarrassing Hans as she scooped him into an embrace and wouldn't let go. My Hans, my son, my darling knabe, my son…Heike stood to one side, looking bored and unhappy but happy he was back all the same. She would see he'd changed. Even a dopey childlike Heike would be able to see he'd changed. Grussie wasn't there. Mutti hadn't told her which train he would arrive on. Otherwise she would have been. They would have looked shyly at each other, asked polite questions, each too shy to broach the delicate subject of what had taken place at Liebenswald, what had transpired, as his Uncle Max was fond of saying, his mother's brother, now at the Front. Dug into a foxhole, looking up over the edge of blistered black frozen earth at the woods the animal would emerge from. Weapon trained on the leafless trees. That's where they'd emerge. The animals. At the first sight of them, he'd squeeze the trigger and one would fall. He'd squeeze again and another animal would collapse, blood running from its mouth. Again. Again. All around Uncle Max, German rifles, machine guns, mortars, brens, artillery…In front of him, piles of Russian animals. And still they would be coming. Coming. More and more. I'm on the platform with Mutti and Heike. Mutti has pulled Heike over to give me a hug. She's insisting we hug. Heike turns so her side faces me and we hug, ten layers of clothes between us, my front to her side. She knows I've changed. She expects what has always been there but she knows that it's gone. Something, she isn't sure what, has taken its place.

.4.

An hour and a half after the trucks left Camp to deliver the Hitler Youth, they returned, loaded with old men from the town of Liebenswald supervised by a handful of SS. The trucks had barely pulled into the dining hall parking lot before its occupants were offloaded and hustled inside. Dr. Shubert, passing from his office to the Library of Aryan and Racial Psychology, paused at this surprising sight and wondered what was happening.

To satisfy his curiosity, Dr. Shubert entered the hall lobby where a variety of banging and clanging noises floated in from the main dining area. Dr. Shubert approached an SS Colonel who explained the entire Camp was being dismantled and that, by the end of the day, it would resemble a ghost town.

Why is this taking place? Dr. Shubert asked, taken aback.

Orders of the Reichfuhrer, the Colonel replied and walked away.

Dr. Shubert remained where he was. A group of four townsmen, carrying a round table top, said Excuse me, please, and Dr. Shubert stepped aside. He watched the men lever the table top down the steps and hoist it, with difficulty, into the back of a transport truck. The sight was so startling that a second group of workmen, carrying a second table top, had to politely ask him twice before he finally moved.

Back outside, Dr. Shubert's first thought was to visit the Camp Commandant. But Lenz had left with the Hitler Youth. He'd said he would. It was his duty to supervise the boys safe return to Berlin. He would ride the train to Berlin and return on the evening express. So Lenz was out. Worried, Shubert wondered if he should consult Dr. Franck. But Franck would know no more than he did. Besides, Franck was not an original thinker. He would worry the subject to death from angles Shubert had exhausted in the first thirty seconds. Better to leave Franck out of it.

The one person Dr. Shubert trusted to give him good advice, he realized as he stepped aside for still more work crews, was his wife. Reversing direction, Dr. Shubert picked up speed as started back toward their thatched roof cottage. At the moment, the snow was still light but the skies had turned deep gray and later it might blizzard. If so, they could be marooned up here, possibly for days.

By the time Dr. Shubert reached the cottage, work crews were everywhere, entering and emerging from houses and dormitories, carrying mattresses and bedding which they piled onto the open beds of the trucks. The mattresses had been stripped and Dr. Shubert couldn't help noticing the stains which disfigured their mid sections. The stains were about eight to twelve inches in diameter and rust colored. Of course, they had been caused by Aryan copulation. Seen like this, however, unmade, uncleaned, there was something undignified, and even sordid, about the mattresses. Dr. Shubert, who normally wasn't that fastidious, wished he hadn't seen them. Not even the prospect of his beloved meerschaum Pipe could quell his uneasiness.

* * *

Gertl was putting up the last of the quince when Dr. Shubert arrived. She smiled at him as always and asked if he would like a cup of coffee. Nonetheless, Dr. Shubert detected an undercurrent of irritation that he'd interrupted her.

No, Dr. Shubert replied. Thank you, Liebschen. I've returned because the Officials are dismantling the Camp.

What do you mean, dismantling?, she asked. What Officials?

Dr. Shubert reached behind him for the seat of a free chair, and lowered himself onto it. They have brought trucks, he explained. They are removing the furniture from all the public rooms. And they are removing the mattresses.

What mattresses? Frau Shubert asked, joining him at the table.

The mattresses where our work came to fruition of course, replied Dr. Shubert. They are piling mattresses into the trucks and they will now truck them away.

Incredible, said Frau Shubert. This is incredible, Fritzl.

Yes. It is, Dr Shubert agreed, reaching for his pipe. He loaded it in silence, tamped the tobacco into the bowl and lit it. Thin blue smoke curled into the dimly lit, cozy kitchen, where a fire roared in the wood stove.

And you were not notified? Frau Shubert offered, rhetorically.

Schatzi, their cat, entered the room, yawned, stretched its back, then took its accustomed place near the stove and stared at its owners, impassively.

What are we going to do? Frau Shubert asked.

Dr Shubert puffed a few times until his face and the table generally were wreathed in fading blue smoke. I am not sure, he replied. Last night's session went off very well, considering the time pressure we put our Youth under. I don't know what they were thinking. Or, I both do and don't, if you know what I mean. You can't expect Youth to perform at the their best when they are told they have only one hour in which to achieve ejaculation, raise their legs to facilitate mitosis, shower, dress, and leave. Such haste is completely against nature. But now of course...

He let his thought trail off. Frau Shubert, more literal than her husband, frowned and patted her hair, wound in braids around her large, placid head. So they already knew, she concluded. Last night. They knew already.

Dr. Shubert nodded as Schatzi jumped onto his lap. Yes, he said, petting the cat. They had at that point already known the Camp was to be evacuated. They knew but did not want to upset the Staff by making it public. So they fabricated the excuse of needing to free the transport trains.

Poor Fritzl, Gertl said, reaching over and covering his mottled hand with her clear, youthful looking one. Should I make you something to eat? Some coffee?

No, said Dr. Shubert sadly. No. I'm fine.

Was the session at least a good one? Frau Shubert ventured after a moment.

Yes. I was surprised, Dr. Shubert reiterated, not bothering to remind her he'd already said this. She was upset. Who could blame her?

Of course, it is too early for you to predict the outcome. I am inquiring only about morale. Was the morale good, liebschen?

They were tired, poor children, said Dr. Shubert. You should have seen them. Some could hardly keep their eyes open. Yet there were others who looked as if they had just come from a conversation with the Fuhrer.

Frau Shubert giggled.

I am not exaggerating, said Dr, Shubert. For them, this has indeed been life altering. Most of them were virgins before the night began. And all of them are idealistic. So idealistic. So it comes as a surprise to them that they are also doing it for themselves. Many have heretofore only masturbated, and some not even that. Imagine, Gertl, what it must have been like for them, their first sexual experience coupled with the knowledge that they are creating our future.

Once more, Gertl patted her husband's hand.

You must be exhausted, she said.

I should be, Yes, said Dr Shubert, but I am not. I am energized.

No? Gertl said with a soft smile, You are not tired?

Realizing she was not speaking about sleep, Dr. Shubert re lit his pipe, and was about to admit he was rather spent when he was preempted by a sharp knock at their door. Dr Shubert and Gertl exchanged glances, and Shubert rose heavily, asking Who is it?

SS, said a rough, urgent voice. We are leaving in one hour. Please to collect your valuables, but only what will fit in a single suitcase. One suitcase to a family, please.

Dr. Shubert opened the door to the black, leather clad backs of two SS walking away from the cottage. What does this mean? he asked.

The older SS turned and fixed Dr. Shubert with a hard stare. We do not have time to repeat ourselves. Pack and assemble at the dining hall in one hour sharp.

Dr. Shubert remained in the doorway a moment, puffing on his pipe. Was it possible this nobody had addressed him in such dismissive fashion? His first impulse was to write down the man's name. But he had answered the door in his slippers. If he walked outside, snow would drench his socks. Furthermore, Dr. Shubert told himself, gradually calming down, if what the insubordinate SS said was true, time was of the essence. Indeed, every second was precious. He and Gertl must now make impossible choices: what to take and what to leave behind.

Back in the kitchen, Shubert found Gertl making selections from her important silver. She held up Angela's baby spoon for his approval and Shubert nodded distractedly. I will go my study, and trust you to see to our domestic keepsakes.

Gertl, always reliable in emergencies, said Go. Go.

Why has the train stopped? Hans asked himself, waking and trying to force his body, wedged between Prusseldorf's and Kline's, to a sitting position. The compartment was silent and full of light. The sun was out.

Hans blinked and looked to his right where Von Stauffenberg wore a serious, almost somber expression.

Where are we? Hans asked. No one replied. He asked a second time, and Prusseldorf shrugged.

What can I possibly leave behind? Dr. Shubert asked himself as he closed the library door and stared at the stacks of files and notebooks that constituted the past two and a half years work. If I take this, I must leave that. But leaving that is inconceivable. Yet if I take that, then I must leave this. Which is equally inconceivable.

Dr. Shubert walked to his desk and opened the topmost file. It contained his latest paper, Race and Blood Knowledge In The Penultimate Generations. He began to read. "The German blood consciousness, first identified by Gerhard Wurmkassen in 1647, runs as vigorously today through the veins of 20th century Lebensborn as it did at that instant in the seventeenth century when Professor Wurmkassen unearthed it." Obviously, this file would have to be saved. So too would that which contained another, as yet un-submitted, paper: The Aryan Dream: How The Aryan Unconscious Unconsciously Exposed The Hidden Jew.

But what of the copious research that had fueled these papers? Research on Blood Knowledge alone would fill a suit-case. It was vital to the inception, not to mention the conception itself, of the Experiment. As were the rows upon rows of books on Race and Genetics and Blood which lined his bookcases. To abandon them would be like abandoning one's children.

For a moment, Hans thought the train's engine had been turned off. But as his brain cleared, he again made out the steady thrum of the pistons as it reverberated through the stopped cars. None of the boys spoke and those who sat away from the windows kept their gazes fastened on Von Stauffenberg and Lars Kestenheim, who had window seats. The latter's' gazes were turned skyward, Kestenheim shielding his eyes with his left hand.

Feeling himself short of breath, Dr Shubert sat down on the couch. He understood the time still available to him was ticking away. He had already wasted a quarter of it. How best to spend that which remained? Suppose he simply left his papers and books in the office? This would mean the Russians would find them and would then possess, among other secrets, the identity of all their Lebensborn offspring. To prevent such a catastrophe, he must burn his papers.

But which papers? Even if he eliminated everything specific to the offspring, a task which could take hours, innumerable memos and notes and genealogies and laboratory reports would remain. Should he by some miracle manage to destroy every relevant paper, a clear impossibility, what of the books themselves? What of his copious marginalia, composed in the certainty that he alone, along with the Reichfuhrer and certain other high Lebensborn officials, would ever see them? Then there were the case files themselves, which filled an entire wall of filing cabinets to the left of the book cases. These must burn too. Everything must burn. If you spared one book, one pamphlet, one monograph, it would point to the existence of a trail. And if Russians, with their well-known animal faculties, caught a scent, they wouldn't rest until they had tracked it down.

Fritz? Are you making progress? Gertl called from downstairs.

Yes, he said. I will be there momentarily.

The strength of his voice surprised him. In this, the darkest moment of his professional life, he was able to summon the professional calm that had so impressed Himmler and by doing so, launched his advance up the ladder of the Lebensborn bureaucracy. And if the outer man sounded calm, Dr. Shubert reasoned, something akin to calm must lie within.

I'm almost finished with the underwear, Gertl reported. I am taking two changes for you and three for me. Will that be enough?

Dr. Shubert nodded but didn't reply. Instead, he rose from the couch and stirred the fire, which sprang to life from this sudden infusion of oxygen. It was odd. Here the final solution to his problems had been staring him in the face for minutes now and he simply couldn't see it. It was if he were searching for his eyeglasses, only to find that he had been wearing them all along.

Opening the filing cases, Dr. Shubert began to lift the heavy manila envelopes from their alphabetical housings and scatter them on the floor. Each envelope spilled from its stiff outer covers dozens of pieces of lined paper, so that, in a matter of moments, the floor was inches deep in birth charts, medical records, psychological inventories, phrenological diagrams, weight graphs, sexual histories, vaccination receipts, and so on. When the first cabinet was completely emptied, Dr. Shubert pulled open the drawers of the second, third, fourth, fifth, and sixth, after which he removed fire screen, ignited a birth chart and, using it as a match, set fire to the loose papers scattered about his feet. The fire spread so rapidly that Dr. Shubert barely had time to rescue his two professional papers before escaping down the stairs.

Gertl, he cried, on reaching the downstairs hallway. Come here immediately.

I am packing our sweaters, Gertl replied.

You will come here this minute! Take what is packed and come here before I come get you.

This was a line from a new game they had invented for their revitalized sex life, one where Gertl, naked, would hide herself in an obscure part of the house while Dr. Shubert tried to find her. Realizing this, Dr. Shubert yelled, This is not a game, Gertl. The house is on fire.

His announcement was met by silence, followed by a gasp, then hurrying footsteps. Smoke was beginning to fill the hallway and the crackling of fire had become audible as it ate away at the library. Dr Shubert put his handkerchief to his nose as Gertl appeared in the hallway, suitcase banging against her thigh. She was saying something over and over, which he couldn't make out.

Come, he cried. Put on your coat and we go.

Are you crazy? she said. Which was what she' d been saying all along. Have you lost your mind?

Dr. Shubert strode into the entryway and removed Gertl's muskrat coat from the coat rack. Here, he said. Put it on.

You have lost your mind, Gertl shrieked, turning to face the fire, which had escaped the library and was creeping along the hall toward the kitchen.

Please do as I say, Dr. Shubert insisted, placing the coat over his wife's shoulders while struggling to wedge her right arm into a sleeve. There will be plenty of time to explain later. Now, we must leave.

.5.

After the train sat on the tracks for thirty-one minutes, SS began to move from compartment to compartment, ordering the Youth to disembark and take up positions on an embankment fifty yards from the idling locomotives. The SS moved quickly, barking orders and closing the doors before they could be asked questions.

Hans again found himself in a slowly oozing river of humanity. When it came turn for him to jump from the steel stairs into the blindingly white snow, he closed his eyes. A spray of powdery white snow hit him in the face. He brushed it aside, opened his eyes, and followed his cadre toward a small rise, on top of which was another set of railroad tracks. Beyond stood dense evergreen forest.

Though many Youth were now conversing with one another, snow damped the sound, adding to the landscape's unreal aspect. Where the Youth had trod, the snow was a crazy quilt of footsteps. But radiating out from the footprints, pristine fields of white stretched to the tree line, uncorrupted by a single set of tracks.

Hans shaded his eyes and stared at the trees, whose limbs held great hats of light, dry snow.

Why are we stopped? Kline asked, in his high pitched, whiny voice.

So you can move your bowels, Kline, Willi said.

Unlike you, I use a toilet for that, von Stauffenberg, Kline replied.

Hans yawned and struggled to stay awake. Nearer the train, a small group of SS conferred with a brakeman. The SS were pointing to something down the tracks. Hans yawned again. In the distance, he heard the unmistakable sound of an approaching train, moving in the direction they had been moving. He squinted at the tracks but could see nothing.

Something's coming, Prusseldorf said, lifting his head so that the sun shone full on his round, characterless face. All the boys were now listening.

Another train, Kline said.

Maybe we have stopped to allow a troop train to pass, said

Kestenheim.

Genius, murmured Willi, causing Kestenheim to blush.

As the train rounded a curve, Hans could see that it was a closed freight, not a troop transport. An SS had run up the embankment where the boys were positioned and was waving his arm back and forth. The approaching locomotive gave three shrill bursts on its whistle by way of answer. The SS waved one last time, then ordered the Hitler Youth to move back from the embankment's summit, which they did.

Hans and the other Youth suddenly understood it was an Undesirables train, carrying prisoners, or maybe even a last wave of Jews. A few Youth began to curse the boxcars, which, odd as it seemed to Hans, gave off the smell of shit. As more Youth joined the cursing, faint cries from the sealed box cars came back in answer. Someone threw a rock, then someone else threw one, then the entire company of Hitler Youth threw rocks and snowballs, which bounced harmlessly off train's wooden sides. Two or three Youth rushed the train, firing their missiles at close range.

The SS shouted at the latter in mock anger, but made no attempt to restore order until an Obersturmfuhrer appeared, shouting for the Youth to relieve themselves where they stood and get ready to return to their compartments. Those Youth who had to shit were to run to the woods, do it as quickly as possible, and return immediately.

Willi, who, like Hans, had watched the train pass in silence, unzipped his fly and removed his penis. He and Hans kept their gaze on the Armed SS, who stood or sat on the roof of the disappearing caboose, submachine guns draped over their knees. One or two saluted, grinning, or so it seemed to Hans.

They smelled like Jews, Kline said, unzipping his fly.

What do Jews smell like? Willi asked, letting go with a powerful stream of urine.

They smell different from Germans, said Prusseldorf, unzipping and re-zipping his fly.

Where are you going, Hercules? Willi asked as Hans started up the embankment. Hans pointed. In reality, he had no need to move his bowels, but ever since Willi commented on the size of his member, Hans felt shy of exposing it. His night with Madchen made him doubly shy. His penis was no longer the innocent, sometimes pleasurable, appendage through which he urinated and which was invariably stiff as a board when he woke from a night's sleep. Something had happened which Hans needed time to absorb.

Ignoring the laughter which rose behind him, Hans scrambled over rails still hot from the passing train and down the other side of the rise where he sank knee deep into fresh snow. The odor of the train had dissolved and the air once again smelled crisp and fragrant with pine. Further back, his own train idled reassuringly, the thump of its engine hypnotic.

Ten yards into the wood, Hans paused, unzipped, and began to urinate. For no particular reason, the act of urinating in fresh air filled him with immense joy. His urine dug a thin, yellow line into the pristine snow, wavering now and then where the wind caught it. The wind on his exposed member felt delicious.

Though Hans was in a hurry to finish...the train wouldn't wait ... he also wanted to remain in this place forever. Somewhere a bird began to sing, then stopped abruptly as unfamiliar sound arose and eclipsed the noise of the idling train. Hans listened, unable at first to identify the sound. It was a plane. Hans plunged from the woods and began to run...he wanted to see the plane. Perhaps it would dip its wings at them. Halfway back, Hans stopped. The approaching plane, he realized, could belong to the enemy. Of course it didn't. It had been sent to make sure they were all right. That, or to prevent sabotage of the train which was carrying Jews. Such mischief had been known to happen. Jews with nothing better to do often set roadblocks for the transports and stormed them, gutting their SS guards and hanging their entrails to cook on the train's engine casings.

Yet as he resumed his walk, Hans was surprised to find that this image, which normally threw him into a rage, had lost its power to affect him. Somehow he had developed a psychological immunity to Jews. The image of the grasping, sycophantic, sexually deranged Hebrew had, if anything,become laughable. It was no more a threat to him, or to those he loved, than any other insect. True, he could...

Hans's thoughts were interrupted by shouting, followed by a thin clacking sound. As the clacking intensified, the shouting became punctuated by screams, some cut off in mid note, some horribly drawn out. Hans took a few more steps, then stopped.

In front of him, a confused mass of Hitler Youth plunged through the snow, racing to get to the train. SS were screaming at them. Other SS had stripped tarps from roof mounted machine guns and were wheeling them skyward.

Out of this sky, Hans, now rooted to his spot, saw a black speck turn and fly toward him. It took only seconds for the speck to resolve into an allied plane, which swooped in low over the snowy fields firing at will. Bodies began to explode. Pieces of matter flew into the air, accompanied by the sound of bullets popping off the metal sides of the passenger cars.

It was over almost before it began. The plane strafed the top of the train one last time, killing several SS, then flew off, becoming smaller in a flash before disappearing completely in the sunlight. Hans stood stunned. His heart was thudding in his chest and, except for the screams, his heart was the only sound he heard. The screams had an unreal quality to them, a staginess, as though they were made by actors rehearsing for a play.

* * *

The trip down the snowy road to the town of Liebenswald took twenty minutes, but to Dr. Shubert and his wife, it felt like an eternity. Looking out the window of their staff car, which they shared with two grim, silent SS, Dr. Shubert tried to distract himself with reflections on the nature of time.

While he and Gertl were standing outside their burning house waiting for the car to collect them, time seemed to stand still. Only the growth of the flames in their house and those surrounding it suggested the world was still temporal and not some immensely large winter-scape. This sensation of time having stopped was of course due to shock, the sudden inability of the human mind to keep pace with external circumstance. But was this inability shock itself, Dr. Shubert wondered, or merely its symptom? The body sustains an injury, whereupon the mind immediately severs its connection to real time, perhaps in an effort to reverse or retract its course.

What happens when the trauma is purely mental, as, for example, when a Jew is removed from his home and herded to a mass assembly point to await the unknown? While you couldn't necessarily extrapolate from a Jew to an Aryan there were enough similarities to use the Jew's experience as a referent. Here too, the issue was the mind's inability to accept reality as defined by what we call the present. One would expect the Jewish race, once it understood what was happening to it, to offer resistance. But, Dr. Shubert reasoned, if his hypothesis was correct, the Jewish race never actually apprehended what was happening. Once the SS knocked on a particular Jewish door, the Jews in question immediately went into a racial shock that denied the existence of both present and future. That is, they entered a state that was nothing more than the inability to apply time, with its intrinsic dependence on cause and effect, to their personal reality.

After adjusting his reading glasses, Dr. Shubert patted himself down for his fountain pen. He would need to take notes if he wanted to be certain he recalled the argument in its original form. Once they arrived at a semi-permanent destination, he could develop the notes into a scientific paper, which he felt certain would be accepted by the Journal Of Racial and Psychological Interrelationships. If the article was as concise and coherent as he believed it would be, it would become a classic.

What is it, Fritzl? Gertl asked. Why are you patting yourself?

What? said Dr. Shubert. I was looking for my pen.

His wife shrugged, and returned to the half-completed sweater she had brought from home and had been obsessively knitting ever since they got in the car. Dr. Shubert watched her a moment, then turned to the SS, who sat stone faced on the opposing seat.

Would either of you happen to have a pen, mein herren? Dr. Shubert said, smiling self-effacingly. For a moment, neither of the SS seemed to have heard. Then the older of the two unbuttoned a breast pocket and, without looking at Dr. Shubert, passed him a fountain pen. Dr. Shubert thanked him and began to look for a piece of paper. Outside, the snow had become heavier and the car's windshield wipers had trouble keeping up with it. The driver, also an SS, drove leaning forward to wipe the fog from the inside of the window with his gloved hand.

How much longer to town? the older SS asked suddenly, peering at the back of the driver's well-trimmed neck.

No more than ten minutes, Leiter, the driver replied.

Do you have any paper? Dr. Shubert asked his wife, who looked up from her lap, blank.

Paper, to write on, dear, Dr. Shubert explained patiently.

But it was no use. Gertl was too deep in shock to process his request. Smiling reassuringly, Dr. Shubert squeezed her stockinged knee and leaned back. He couldn't very well ask the SS for paper, having just asked them for a pen. This would make him, what was the Yiddish word for it? A schnorrer. Yes, that was it, a schnorrer, a word he had learned from a Hebrew colleague while both were students in medical school. Schnorrer: someone who constantly borrows things from others, possibly failing to return them in the bargain. To borrow was one thing, part of the everyday economy of human life. To habitually borrow things you should have bought for yourself meant you were a schnorrer, a person who, having nothing of his own, was parasitically dependent on those who had what he didn't. It was no wonder the Jews invented this word. It described them to a tee.

Kupferberg. Louis Kupferberg. That was his colleague's name. At the time – this was before Dr. Shubert had become a convert to the party—Kupferberg had seemed unremarkable enough, neither more nor less memorable than any other medical student. True, he had an odd shaped head, coming to a rather pronounced point at the top. But most Jewish heads were oddly shaped. It was a racial characteristic, the way a flat nose was a racial characteristic of the Negro, or flat cheeks a characteristic of the Slavic untermensch.

Dr. Shubert glanced at Gertl, who continued to fiddle with her half-knit sweater, then glanced out his window. They were nearing Liebenswald. A few houses passed by on either side of the car, their outlines blurred by the blowing snow. It was odd, Dr. Schubert mused, what one remembered and what one didn't He hadn't seen or thought of Kupferberg for twenty five years, yet his memory was stored and ready to be pressed into service at the drop of a hat. Kupferberg had been studying surgery, unlike Dr. Shubert who knew early on he wanted to be a psychiatrist. Not a Jewish psychiatrist, of course. An Aryan psychiatrist, whose theoretical groundwork lay in the exercise of Will, the combination of Race and Will.

Kupferberg's problem was his height. He was very tall. Six

inches taller than Dr. Shubert. He had the habit of bending over when he listened to you, as though he were hard of hearing. Which might explain his head. There wasn't enough life force in his body to reach the head. So it grew anomalously.

Just as Dr. Shubert smiled, the driver cursed out loud and the SS tensed up in their seats. Dr. Shubert had the sensation of gliding, as though the car had suddenly begun to ice skate. Gertl grabbed his bicep and held on tight. Had she said something? Dr. Shubert didn't think so. The driver continued to curse and spin the wheel, but the car continued its slide, as though it had suddenly divorced itself from the physics that normally governed its motion.

What's happening? Gertl cried. Why is he doing this?

Dr. Shubert wanted to comfort her but was equally reluctant to do anything which might make her make a scene. He might have said Squirrel, or Cat, to explain the car's behavior. The driver swerved to avoid a puppy and momentarily lost control. If we're patient, he will regain control and we will be on our way. We will be put up for the night...the car hit some saplings and now spun in circles as it drifted toward the far side of the road ...by Liebenswalders. For one night, we will be schnorrers, like my young colleague, Dr. Kupferberg. What had he borrowed, Dr. Shubert wondered as the car hit a snow-covered oak producing a deep thud. Gertl was now screaming. Dr. Shubert reached for her hand, but, thrown off balance, dug his hand into her crotch instead. She screamed louder. Across from them, the SS were gripping hand straps set into the columns between front and back windows.

What did he borrow from me? Dr. Shubert asked himself, breathing rapidly, and seeking relief from this distraction. The road was icy. The car's ping ponging could go on for some time. Normally this would be harmless. They were in a heavily armored Mercedes. Little could happen, apart perhaps from a few bruises. Had he borrowed money? Unlikely. Even then, during his years of relative innocence, Dr Shubert was too sophisticated to loan money to a Jew. It must have been some-thing else. A pen, perhaps. Or a book. Yes. That was it. It was probably a book. Kupferberg had probably said, I don't want to be a schnorrer, but could you possibly lend me X? And he would have asked what schnorrer meant, and Kupferberg would have replied, someone who is forever borrowing...

Again, a protracted yet silent slide ended with a thud, as the car, now facing uphill, in the direction of the camp, began to slide backwards, picking up speed. The driver cursed steadily, his guttural glottals competing with Gertl's veolars and the SS's grim silence. Haskell Kupferberg. That was his name. Not Louis. Or Leibish, as the Jews fashioned it. Haskell. Haskell Kupferberg. Dr. Shubert reached up and grabbed his own strap, willing himself to relax into the next collision. Haskell Kupferberg. He had the room across the hall from mine. I used to go in there in the morning, whenever I smelled coffee. He made the most delicious...

Dr. Shubert colored. He'd had it backwards. It wasn't Kupferberg who borrowed things from him. It was he who'd borrowed them from Kupferberg. Kupferberg, he now recalled, had come from a rich merchant family which was continually sending him packages of exotic coffees and fruits and sausages. He, Dr. Fritz Shubert, was in the habit of strolling across the hall to Kupferberg's room in order to share in these riches. That was how he came to know the word Schnorrer...THUD... Kupferberg had used it in relation to him.

* * *

The remainder of the trip home began in complete silence. Surviving Hitler Youth were told to retake their original seats and Hans dutifully took his between Willi and Prusseldorf. He had been sitting between Prusseldorf and Kline, but Kline now lay in the caboose with the other dead.

For what seemed like hours, no one spoke. As the trip wore on, Willi began to cadge cigarettes from his compartment mates. His had been lost in the snow. Prusseldorf loaned Willi two cigarettes, but said he would loan him no more until these two were returned, which struck Hans as absurd but also, as not worth mentioning.

Did I ask you to loan me more? Willi asked.

The rest are exclusively mine and therefore, for me alone, Prusseldorf said, clutching his crushed pack.

Aren't you afraid someone might call you a Jew for hoarding?

Willi said.

It would be you who was the Jew, interjected a small, perfectly featured Hitler Youth who sat by the window and whom Hans didn't recognize. Jews borrow things, but neglect to return them.

I beg your pardon, Willi said, with exaggerated politeness. I am tenth generation German nobility. My family can trace its history back to William the Conqueror...

William the Conqueror was English swine, said the Youth.

So the English would have you believe, Willi countered. Just as they would have you believe Russians are descended from the Jewish race. In fact, there is no love lost between Russians and Jews. Russians narrowly escaped becoming Jews in the 14th Century. After which, they turned on them and have kept turning ever since.

What are you talking about? Asked the sharp featured boy. You are talking complete crap.

Hans watched Willi blow a long plume of smoke into the air. Willi, he realized, was as upset as he was by what had happened, but would die before he showed it. This was what made Willi a leader. Nothing disturbed his surface. He remained the same, sardonic, fearless gadfly no matter what. For this, people looked up to him.

When Tsar Nicholas II, Willi continued, began shopping for a new religion, he narrowed the candidates to two: Jews and, excuse me....Willi sneezed...the Greek Orthodox Church. He chose Greek Orthodox, which, as you know, later became Russian Orthodox, and this remained the official religion of Russia until it was banned by the anti-Christ; but for a few hair-raising moments, in the 14th century, so far as the Jews were concerned, it was touch and go.

The small Hitler Youth had long since looked away and didn't respond.

When it became clear the dialog was at an end, Willi wrapped his arms around his chest, closed his eyes, and fell asleep, leaning his full weight against Hans's side. Hans tried to free himself, but the Hitler Youth to Willi's right had also fallen asleep, and Willi was immovable.

Slowly, the train built speed. Hans looked out a window as countryside whizzed by, punctuated at intervals by small towns.

The towns looked like mutes, buried as they were in snow; yet Hans sensed something inviting in them. Blue smoke trickled from their chimneys as if to say, Come in, it's warm inside.

The precise featured Hitler Youth had awakened and was also looking out the windows, his chin cupped in his hand. He looked older than he was. He was one of those people who had always looked old, in spite of his smallish size. This was what led him to confront Willi. He had never felt the insecurities that go with being young.

Yet, Hans wondered, as his leg began to jerk up and down of its own accord, had this young Hitler Youth been able to achieve climax with his Lebensborn partner? Hans thought not. The two would have spent their time discoursing on politics, or racial theory, or the war effort. Not that the precise featured boy was afraid or disobedient. He was just too young. To successfully conclude his mission, as Hans and Willi had, one must have physical maturity, a prick that could defy gravity, and the will to keep going.

(Hans wished someone would stop screaming.)

In all fairness, however, it was a pity about the small Hitler Youth. Other than his size and age, he had what the program was looking for. He was blonder than Hans or Willi. He possessed features which suggested impeccable genetic credentials. And he had tremendous self-confidence. Had he been able to mate, he would have produced a prototype for the next five hundred years. But he hadn't. Hans was certain of this. Look at the way he held himself --rigid, immobile, as if he were a painting. Had he achieved climax with a female, he would have relaxed, as Hans had. Hans was now completely relaxed. Even the pain…

Those Hitler Youth who had had successful congress with young women were by and large, ordinary. Compared to Slavs, of course, they were gods. Even dozing with their mouths open, their heads thrown back, they seemed self-possessed… in control. They were the best of the best. Their progeny would exceed even their capacities. Meaning, Hans inferred, though this felt rather vague, his own would too. His and Madchen's son would carry in him genes which had been pre-selected for greatness. Just as successful congress between lion and lioness would produce lion cubs, that between Hitler Youth and healthy, intelligent, German countrywomen would produce gods. Hans coughed and asked for a glass of water.

Prusseldorf? Produce a god? Hans heard Willi mock him. But Willi was asleep. He must have talked in his sleep. To produce a god, Hans thought, it didn't necessarily have to have only to do with you. With who, then? Willi demanded.

With the Program. The Program, Hans replied, is larger its than parts. It is an idea. An idea is always greater...Hans paused to catch his breath; the train speed was bothering him...than the sum of its parts. The German Race, for instance. If we were not greater than the sum of our parts, how could we have conquered the entire world?

The perfect featured boy snickered. Hans reddened with fury, but kept his peace. He felt light headed, as though there were two of him: he, and his body. He must be terribly tired. He was terribly tired. Too tired to sleep. But neither did he want to sleep. He wanted to think about Frau Unger, but she eluded him too. He glimpsed her fat, flat white buttocks, shaking above her sheer black stockings so he pinched and slapped them. But they disappeared.

How, he wondered, does a rump that size disappear? You'd be surprised, Willi said, as if he could read Hans's thoughts.

Doesn't anyone have a glass of water? Hans asked.

You can go to the lavatory, the perfect featured boy said, but you'll have to step over the SS. They're sleeping in the corridor.

No, they aren't, Hans said.

Yes they are, said the boy. They sleep sitting up.

Never!, Hans replied, louder than he should have. He was so angry, he had trouble focusing on the boy, who remained as calm as ever.

There was something Hans wanted to think about but he couldn't remember what. Grussie? No. He didn't want to think about Grussie just now. Her smile was too ironic. Would he really want a child with that smile? No. He would have to discuss it with her. If they were going to spend their lives together, she would have to change her smile. Become more like Madchen, more accepting and matter of fact. Madchen was an angel. She thought nothing of taking his penis in her mouth to make it hard. He had never ever known that girls did such a thing. Only Jewesses. No one would call Frau Unger a girl.

Not in your wildest dreams.

Hans spent a few moments simply listening to the train. It plowed ahead, moving at a steady pace. Hans knew he should close his eyes and sleep, but he was too uncomfortable. And there were things to resolve. Now that he was a father, should he continue seeing Frau Unger? The answer was clear. It would be unethical for a German father to visit a Jewess, no matter what the circumstances. That settled it. He would give Frau Unger up. And Grussie?

This was different. He loved Grussie. He must tell her of course, that he'd become a father. She would be hurt. She would turn for consolation to her mother, who, Hans suspected, had reservations about him. She might be a Jewish sympathizer.

No, this wasn't possible, Hans realized, pausing to cough up phlegm. She dislikes Jews more than I do. Still, what if her dislike was an act to divert suspicion? Do you remember when she came into the living room as Grussie and I were kissing? This is exactly what a Jewish mother would do. Listen for silence, and immediately suspect the worst. Which is why their children grew up so pale and unhealthy looking. They were never allowed to be themselves. Only by being yourself can your blood circulate in a healthy fashion. Jews were not interested in blood. They were interested in money. In sucking blood. Not enriching it with courage and unflinching ...unflinching...unflinching...

What are you raging about, Hercules? Willi asked, waking, but still leaning heavier than ever against Hans's left side.

Nothing. Shut up, Hans replied.

Are you upset about the air raid? Willi continued. Because, that was nothing. It seemed important because our Comrades were killed, yet in reality...

No. Fuck yourself, Hans said, suddenly hating Willi.

Without straightening up, Willi removed a cigarette from behind his ear and lit it. He inhaled deeply and exhaled with pleasure, producing an endless stream of smoke which rose from his head, now resting on Hans's chest, to Hans's nose. Hans coughed and turned away. He waited for Willi to run out of breath, but it seemed as if the smoke would pour out forever. At last, it stopped and Willi again drew on the cigarette.

One must steel oneself to look these things in the face, Willi continued. At first, Hans thought he was talking about

Madchen's vagina and began to laugh, a laugh however that quickly turned into a cough. This is simply what we are made of. Normally we never get to see this because that is how civilized life is conducted: it is conducted to conceal from us what lies beneath our skin.

Hans willed himself to relax. He understood Willi was trying to comfort him, and part of him appreciated this and was grateful for it. But another part wanted to be alone with his thoughts. He wanted to stop seeing Kline's eyes following him as he passed. This was intolerable. It was Kline's duty to accept his position no less than it was Hans's to accept his. If he had been in Kline's place...

Here was Frau Unger again. He must do something about her. The train had begun to pick up speed. There was no interval between wheel revolutions. Merely a steady, iron whir. Hans closed his eyes. He had left the woods at the first sign of the Spitfire and it passed directly over his head. For a split second, its shadow covered his entire body. The shadow came racing across the snow, then covered and passed him. Then disappeared, but turned and came back. A dot at first, then larger and larger. Someone had pushed him into the snow. Willi? Prusseldorf? He couldn't visualize who had pushed him. A hard push. Like a blow. The SS? A trail of bullets punched past his snow bound head, but he remained alive.

When Hans awoke from his nap, it was dark. The lights in the compartment were off so as not to give away the train's position. Outside, the darkness was also unbroken by lights. Everything was blacked out; you couldn't make out the snow which was falling swiftly past the train's windows.

His compartment mates were still asleep and Hans let his gaze rove from one dim body to another. To his surprise, he felt a sudden, overpowering love for them. Even for the perfect featured boy, who now slept with his mouth open, the dried bloodstains on his tunic in marked contrast to the surreal whiteness of his face and hair. They had all survived, he, Willi, Prusseldorf. Had Prusseldorf survived? Yes. There he was. That wasn't snow outside. It was buildings. They were passing buildings. A long line of them, all dark. Dark buildings, lit by the blue light at the front of the train. The only light.

Hans felt stronger. More composed. He rubbed his eyes.

The tears had dried on his face and gave his skin a roughened feel. That's right. He had been crying. No one saw, however. No one would know. It was all right too to cry over the death of those you loved. Even though he hadn't loved them. Any more than he loved: who? One thing was certain, there were no longer any Jews. They now had other tasks. That one was thankfully complete. There were no longer Jews. True, other forms of low life were taking their place. But we will defeat those too. We will throw them out. Throw them back. Bury them. The weak have numbers. There are always more of them. The weak and degenerate.

The leg was pumping again. But at least the train was slowing. Unmistakably. It was going slower. You could tell by the speed with which the buildings were passing. The snow too seemed lighter. Even with your eyes closed, you could tell the train was slowing. He would see Grussie tomorrow. Or write to her. He'd already said goodbye. It was unmanly to say goodbye twice. But he wanted to see her. Explain. Then...off to war.

He touched the dried blood on his chest and found it had inexplicably become wet. His fingers came away sticky. This was odd. The compartment too was different. There was more room. He was lying down in it, and someone had turned off the heat because it was now very cold. And the lights were on. They had turned on the lights. They were extremely bright, as if he were on an operating table, like when he had his tonsils out, just before they gave him ether and he saw and heard and felt nothing.

.6.

Hush, Julia said to Heike, holding a finger to her lips for emphasis. Come in. Quickly. Don't make any noise.

Why not? Whispered Heike.

I don't want them to know you're here. So be quiet.

You don't want who to know? asked Heike, stumbling over the Persian runner.

My parents. Will you be quiet?

Not know what? Heike asked in a whisper.

Julie pushed her into her bedroom and closed the door. Then she turned and stared at Heike, who was now seated on the bed.

I did it, Julia said.

Did what? Heike asked, knowing full well what she meant.

With Damian Kronenshecker.

You mean..., Heike gasped.

Julia glanced around as though someone else might be in the room. Then she came and sat down beside her friend.

When? Heike asked, breathless.

Yesterday afternoon. At his house.

No, Heike said. Scandalized. Horrified.

Not so loud, said Julia. His parents were away. His father is a doctor. He's experimenting with prosthetics.

What are prosthetics? Heike asked, studying Julia for visible signs of transformation. To Heike's surprise, and disappointment, she looked exactly the same as before.

You know. Wooden limbs. His mother works as a nurse. She was a nurse even before his father married her. That's how they met.

Did it hurt?

No. Yes, said Julia. A little. Not as much as I thought though. I brought a wooden spoon to put between my teeth...

Was it disgusting? Heike couldn't prevent herself from asking.

A little, Julia admitted. Anyway, it's done. So if I die, at least I did it. You should...

Someone knocked on the door and the girls froze. The door opened and Frau Oberlacher appeared, smiling at them. Her hair was up and she looked like an old young girl.

Oh. Here you are, Frau Oberlacher said without coming in. How about a nice cup of hot chocolate.

Heike looked at Julia for permission.

Don't look at Julia. She has hot chocolate every day, Frau Oberlacher observed. I'll make you both a cup. It's snowing, so it will be perfect.

Thanks, Mutti, Julia said without enthusiasm.

Thank you, Frau Oberlacher, Heike said, meaning it.

You're welcome, dear Frau Oberlacher said. Oh, and by the way, you can take your coat off. We have heat today.

Close the door when you leave please, Mutti, Julia said.

But why? asked Frau Oberlacher.

We're talking about boys.

Heike giggled. Frau Oberlacher gave them a look, rolled her eyes, but closed the door anyway. They heard her sigh as she walked off.

Heike stared at her friend with awe.

Did it...you know.

Bleed? Julia guessed. Uh huh. A little. Not too much. I expected it to bleed more so I brought a lot of gauze. A whole bagful. But I didn't need it. You should have seen me. My knapsack looked like a suitcase.

I want to know what happened, so tell me everything, Heike said, but don't tell me details because I don't want to know those. Just tell me, you know, how it felt and if you wanted to do it again and if you thought you might die.

Julia nodded and brushed hair off her forehead.

So...First, we had to make sure no one was home. He went in and called to his parents, then I went in. They have a big apartment on Gunther Hoppen Platz. Three bedrooms. One less than ours. But only one bathroom.

He has his own room?

Yes, but we used a towel anyway, in case the maid told his parents about the sheets.

Towel for what? Heike whispered in a scream. She couldn't believe they were having this conversation. At the same time, she would have died rather than stop before she knew everything.

So the blood wouldn't stain them, stupid. Anyhow, he closed

the door and...No, first he asked me if I wanted something to drink. I said No. He said he did, so he poured himself schnapps from his father's liquor cabinet. I said I was going to go get undressed. He said we had time and asked if I wanted to listen to music first...They have a Victrola...but I said No. I was eager to get it over with.

No!, Heike cried. You actually said that?

So he said, Okay, and started to get undressed. I wanted to undress by myself so I asked him where the bathroom was and took off my clothes there.

What happened when you went out? Heike asked, scandalized that Julia might have walked through a strange apartment naked.

I covered myself with a towel and got into bed the instant I got back. I was nervous about being naked in front of a boy. You have a brother, but it was my first time. Guess what happened the second I got into bed? Julia continued, whispering excitedly.

What? shrieked Heike.

We heard bombers, Julia said. Both of us thought it was an air raid. We jumped out of bed and he looked for his pants when we realized there were no air raid sirens. As soon as we realized it, we started to laugh. That's when I remembered I was naked. He was almost naked. His thing was sticking straight out from his underwear. It was this big.

Julia illustrated.

Heike put a hand over her mouth.

What did you do? she asked

I got back into bed with my eyes closed. I said to myself, it's now or never. You could die tonight. Do you want to do it, or not? Then he got into bed and I opened my eyes. He was nervous too. He kept putting his hands under the cover, touching his thing and I told him to stop. I'd do it. So I reached under the covers and...

A Refreshment Interlude.

Mitzi, the maid, hadn't come to work due to illness, so Frau Oberlacher made the hot chocolate herself. Here is her recipe: Gently heat the milk.

Grate dark chocolate, (NEVER MILK CHOCOLATE!), put up several spoonfuls of sugar, a sprinkling of orange zest, and a soupcon of brandy, no more.

When a skin begins to form on the milk's surface, you must act decisively.

Remove the milk from burner, stir in chocolate a little at a time, making certain each spoonful is fully dissolved before adding the next.

Once the milk and chocolate have bonded, stir in sugar, being careful to add it slowly so that it blends. Then add the brandy all at once, sprinkle with zest and serve.

A Note Concerning Temperature

It's important to remember that cooling will begin immediately on removal of the pot from the stove-top. Therefore, as important as it is not to rush, it is equally important to move with dispatch. You want to serve your hot chocolate hot, not at room temperature. This argues for having your ingredients at the ready beforehand.

A Note Concerning China

Many preparers make the mistake of serving their hot chocolate, (now no longer available to the general public although it remains a treat for high ranking military and party officials), in mugs. Nothing could be worse for hot chocolate. The mug's thick surface absorb heat and quickly leaches warmth from the hot chocolate. This is true even when the mug has been heated beforehand.

To avoid this, serve your hot chocolate, where feasible, in bone china. Not only will bone china not absorb heat; it will distribute the heat evenly from top to bottom.

In the Kitchen

How is it? Frau Oberlacher inquires.

It's wonderful, Frau Oberlacher, Heike says, bright red.

Slowly Heike, Frau Oberlacher says. Drink slowly. We do not want people to think we are trying to set you on fire.

Are you going out, Mutti? asked Julia.

No, said Frau Oberlacher, If you knew how much I have to do. We are having company to dinner. Your father has invited the Minister of Domestic Transportation, and Father Peter, (here addressing Heike) He used to be our Priest until he saw the Truth and joined the Party. Oh, and Elspeth Frickler and her mother, Johanna. These are the iron and steel Fricklers, Heike, Frau Oberlacher adds, smiling maternally, if a bit patronizingly, the Fricklers who own that island in the River.

Heike nodded, stupidly, she felt.

Is iron and steel what you're feeding them for supper, Mutti? Or do they bring that as a gift? Julia interjects, wide eyed with mock curiosity.

Jul...yah, Frau Oberlacher warns.

Mutti...Julia mocks her.

Heike sips her hot chocolate and feels it print a moustache on her upper lip.

In the Street

The first thing Heike noticed coming out of Julia's building was that it had stopped snowing. A few flurries here and there but the sky was now steely blue and the clouds had all but disappeared. Heike squinted and pulled her scarf tight around her neck to protect against the fierce wind. Snow still blew at her, but now only from the snow-covered ground.

Traditionally, Heike liked snow. She liked the magical transformation of one world into another. The gray, stupid buildings were still gray and stupid but you wouldn't see them anymore. Instead, a veil of grayish white was pulled over them, a veil that rose and fell and billowed and sank back depending on the wind. When she was younger, Heike would sit at her window for hours staring at the falling snow. This was before the move to the Rosenfelds. Once in her new bedroom, for some reason she lost the desire to look at the snow. Of course, she was older. Plus, there was a war going on. Although, to be honest, she was still fascinated by snow when the war began. But they hadn't yet been bombed.

Heike remembered the exact day and time the war arrived. She was walking back from Mochwelt's grocery store with cheese and butter when the air suddenly filled with sirens. Initially, no one knew what was happening. Heike was the first to run into a building and down the stairs to the basement, as her Aryan History teacher, Frau Kauthenschaaft, had instructed them to. Heike detested Frau Kauthenschaaft but for some reason had complete recall of the day she warned the class that the enemy might someday bomb their houses. Gudrun Sicherheit had raised her hand and said that her father had said that there was no chance the enemy would ever bomb them because the Luftwaffe was a far superior fighting force and would die rather than let enemy planes enter German air space.

Frau Kauthenschaaft turned red and said of course it was true that German air power was superior to that of our enemies, just as it was true that German land forces had acquitted themselves well in the ground war. But the girls had an obligation, as young Aryan women, to preserve bodies and their health in the event, unlikely as it was, that an Allied plane got through.

This was five years ago. Yet even at age eight, Heike had known enough to dart into a building while everyone else was standing in the street with their mouths open. She'd tripped down the stairs to the basement, which was open, but dark and smelly and probably full of rats and insects. Heike stood in the dark, trembling, until other people gradually filtered in – some from the building and others from the streets outside. After a while, they heard the planes arrive, a low whir, followed by an increasingly loud hum, followed by a steady roar punctuated now and then by explosions which sounded like paper bags popping.

When it was all over, and they knew this because the All Clear sounded, Heike had gone up onto the street and seen her first fires. Huge sections of a nearby street were on fire and Heike had watched, fascinated, as fire trucks and other vehicles sped to the scene. In a way, it was thrilling. All that equipment and all those men, rushing to one place with only one purpose: to put out the fire and save people. On the other hand, it was frightening because, what if the bombs had fallen on her building. Would she even be alive to worry about it?

From Julia's house, Heike turned left, and started across Uber Platz toward Brandenburg Strasse, which she had decided to take, instead of her usual route, which was Haydn Strasse to Erlacher Platz to Marien Strasse. She didn't reflect on why she was doing this. She just was. Maybe it was the sun. Haydn Strasse had particularly large apartment buildings, two of which had been destroyed, and the sun had difficulty filtering down to the pavement. Besides, most of the residents of Haydn Strasse were old, old men as well as old women, and Heike wasn't in the mood for old people. Normally, she liked old people, or at least had nothing against them. Even Herr Gruber, who she knew for a fact was always looking for an excuse to peek under her skirt. It was gross but he probably couldn't help it. All males wanted to look under girls' skirts. That's how God made them, apparently, though why He did mystified her.

The sun had the curious effect of making the snow appear silver. It glittered and wore a silvery sheen, right up to the second Heike kicked it and it would blow up, light and powdery. Some of the things she'd discussed with Julia she'd already repressed. For example, she couldn't remember what Julia had said about Damien Kronenschecker's thing. The whole business of boys' things was mystifying. If God existed, and could do anything He wanted, why couldn't he think of a better way for people to produce babies than that? Plus, why make the baby grow inside the woman for nine months? Why not two months, or three, tops? Why have another person inside you for nine months? And why only women? Why didn't men have babies?

All these questions, of course, had answers. Julia knew most of them. When God made people, he handed off the business of reproduction. Before Eve ate the apple, which Heike didn't believe, children were going to be born without causing their mothers pain. It was only after the apple that everything bad happened.

Including...you know? Heike recalled having asked in a whisper, though it wasn't necessary to whisper since Julia's room sat at the end of a long hallway and was furnished with lots of heavy furniture. Still, she didn't want to take the chance Frau Oberlacher might overhear her. And the prospect of Herr Oberlacher, with his rimless eyeglasses and cold, green stare catching wind of their discussion horrified her. Much as she loved Julia, Herr Oberlacher gave her the creeps. And since he was a male, Herr Oberlacher had one too. Heike couldn't bear to think he'd used it on Frau Oberlacher, but Julia and her siblings were living proof he had.

Plus, Heike continued, aren't you scared you might, you know...

Stop ending every sentence with You know, Julia ordered. It makes me dizzy. No, I'm not scared because we used protection.

What do you mean, protection? Heike had asked.

Julia had rolled her eyes and opened a desk drawer, from which she retrieved, from under a pile of papers, envelopes, erasers, and rubber bands, which were now almost completely unavailable due to rubber shortages, a round disc which she held up by its thickened rim.

What's that? Heike asked.

A diaphragm, Julia replied, knowingly.

What's it for?

You put it in you and it stops the sperm from going up, Julia said, replacing it in its hiding place.

Put it where? Heike said, then turned scarlet and said, You're joking.

Recalling their conversation now, from the far side of Uber Platz, where the sun was so intense Heike had to shade her eyes with one hand, it seemed to her that Julia had answered her question by lifting her skirt and plunging the round object toward her place. This couldn't have happened. For all her daring, Julia was refined and cultured. She played Beethoven on the piano. Before the war, live string quartets had played in the family apartment, though once war broke out, the Jewish parts of the quartet had been sent away. Julia said this out loud, boldly and casually, daring anyone to make something of it. Of course, no one did, knowing who her father was.

Once through the Square and into Gras Strasse, the sun became less intense and Heike was more able to focus on her surroundings. Gras Strasse itself had been heavily bombed.

Just off Uber Platz, three buildings were reduced to rubble and a work gang moved in and out of the second of the three carrying pieces of brick and concrete which they dumped into a waiting Army Truck. The work gang was made up of prisoners, probably Russian, since they were brown eyed and emaciated. For some reason, Julia reported that her father had said, the Russian prisoners wouldn't eat, although he'd winked as he said it.

As she came level with the work gang, one of the prisoners glanced at her. Heike quickly looked away. The man's face was so thin his eyes seemed the only thing that kept it from collapsing. Instead of disgust, however, Heike felt pity. She dug in her pocket for a piece of bread, but all she found were the three caramels Julia had given her for dessert, one each for her, Hans, and Mutti. She could give the man Hans's caramel, but then all the other prisoners would want one. This was the trouble with trying to do something good. If you did it for one person, other people expected you to do it for them too.

Heike picked up her pace and passed the three SS who were guarding the work gang. The SS said something and laughed. Heike had to work to persuade herself they weren't laughing at her. Just because they laughed as she passed didn't mean they were laughing at her.

Ahead, a small convoy of personnel trucks was parked at an intersection. They looked empty. Everyone had gotten used to seeing them. Heike wondered what it would be like to ride in one. If it was snowing, snow would come right into the back. In summer, though, there would be a breeze.

The slight nausea she always felt when she left Julia's was coming back. This was because, while Frau Oberlacher always gave them sweets, she never gave them real food. The sweets fell on an empty stomach and made her a little sick. Given a choice between whether or not to have one, however, Heike would have always chosen the sweet. Peeling the paper off the sticky surface of a caramel was one of the best things in the world. Unless the candy had come from Herr Gruber. Even then, it was good. Sucking on a candy helped you relax as the bombers approached your block. Not only did it address your hunger, it gave you something to do. Certain kinds of Herr Gruber 's candy you could bite down on. Those were the best. You had to endure Herr Gruber looking at you with his gross old man's smile, but all in all it was worth it. Besides, Herr Gruber wasn't so bad all the time. Just when you sat down or stood up and he tried to look under your skirt. Or when he made jokes about the Jews. It was almost always the same joke now that the weather was bad. He would say, It's raining cats and dogs and Jews outside. And when she would say nothing, he would ask, Don't you want to know why it's raining Jews. And when Heike, to be polite, would nod, he would say, Because even Heaven doesn't want them.

Maybe it had been funny the first time. It wasn't funny the twentieth. It probably hadn't even been funny the first time. Herr Gruber couldn't stop laughing at it. He would throw his head back and hold his stomach and laugh, then look down at you through squinty eyes and say, No? You get it, Liebeschen? Because he was old, Heike would always muster a little smile. And also because they were the first two to the shelter. Herr Gruber probably lived in the shelter, Heike thought and giggled. Ahead, two tanks rolled through the intersection, as though they were driving themselves, while on the other side of the street, more collapsed buildings became visible.

If you had told her, Heike mused, jumping over what used to be wooden beams, five years ago that she would one day be walking past bombed out buildings without even looking at them, she would have thought you'd lost your mind. But here she was doing just that. The buildings to either side of the ruined one stood completely unaffected, as though the bomb had deliberately wiped out the middle building but chosen not to touch those to the left or right. Their scrolled windows and gargoyle tops looked as solid and grim as ever, Heike thought, looking up, then down again. But you couldn't know what would happen. Tonight they might drop another bomb and tomorrow, this building wouldn't exist.

The same could happen to her building, Heike knew, vaulting a small hill of snow covered bricks lying in the middle of side-walk. Usually these were cleared by the next day, so maybe the debris was from yesterday. Two older women approached from the other direction. Heike said Good Day to them and hopped off the sidewalk to let them pass. They smiled at her politeness and said Good Day back. One of them stopped, reached in a bag and called to her.

Here, Liebschen, she said, handing Heike a small onion.
Heike stared at the onion, now nestled in her mitten, and
wanted to say No, thank you, but couldn't.

Give it to your mother to cook, child, the woman said, patting
her on the shoulder and moving off.

An onion was like a…a gift from God, Heike thought. No one
gave onions away. Maybe it was poisoned. Maybe the woman
was a Jew, was getting back at Aryans by handing out poisoned
onions. Heike knew this was ridiculous. There were no more
Jews, and if there were, they weren't on Gras Strasse giving
onions to unsuspecting Aryans. The woman must have liked her.
She must have had enough onions to afford to give one away.

Heike put the onion in her pocket and wiped away some
tears. The onion must have made them water, she thought,
knowing full well that that wasn't it. But it felt good to cry at
the woman's generosity. In fact, at the moment, everything
felt good. It felt good to have talked to Julia and hear her
description, rendered in clinical detail, of the horrible thing she
had allowed Damian Kronenscheker to do to her. It felt good to
have the hot chocolate. It felt good to have a debate with herself
over the nature of God and whether or not he was benevolent.
"Benevolent" was a word their Racial Theory teacher, Fraulein
Pfuttenpfeffer, liked to use with reference to the Fuhrer. A benevolent Fuhrer was one who loved and looked out for his people,
she would say, and their Fuhrer was a benevolent Fuhrer.
Whenever she said this, her face would take on a rapturous,
far-away look, and Julia, who sat next to Heike in Racial Theory,
never overlooked the opportunity this provided to poke Heike in
the shoulder or side.

Even the cold felt good. It reminded her of the days Mutti
used to take her and Hans sledding in the park. She hadn't
thought about Hans for a whole half day now, but suddenly
remembered what it felt like to sit behind him on the sled,
screaming and clutching him around his middle as the sled
raced downhill. He would be screaming too, wouldn't he? Or
would he? There was always something somber about Hans,
something that wouldn't let him scream with pleasure. Heike
couldn't help wondering if he screamed with pleasure when he
was…

Despite the fact no one was looking, she blushed and

kicked up a storm of powdery snow to cover her embarrassment. Ahead was another bombed out building, this one with sawhorses guarding its perimeter. Sawhorses too had become a familiar sight, beginning with the eviction of the Jews. Heike remembered seeing lines of Jews being pointed by SS toward makeshift pathways marked off by sawhorses. The Jews had moved slowly, everyone but the children carrying suitcases. They couldn't move fast because there were always lots of Jews moving slowly in front of them. Leisl Mann said Jews moved slowly because they never exercised and their leg muscles wouldn't allow them to walk quickly, but Heike didn't believe it. Leisl had been killed when the building across the street from theirs collapsed. Heike hadn't liked her but remembered crying when she heard the news. She wondered if she was prone to crying.

She decided she wasn't. She hadn't cried over the Jews, not even when the children looked at her. They looked frightened. Of course, this was because they were leaving home and didn't know where they were going. Children hated change. She herself had hated it when she was little. Now she dreamed of going to new places. She was especially enamored of the idea of going to America. In America, Julia said, girls could do everything. Become doctors. Go to university. Drink and smoke.

Another reason she hadn't cried when the Jews were expelled was, the SS was always there, mostly looking at them, but occasionally looking at you too. In fact, she had wanted to cry, particularly when they removed the Jews from their street. Heike hadn't realized there were so many Jews on this block of Vielenstrasse. Over a hundred. Maybe more. Some of the Jews looked normal but most of them, if you looked hard enough, looked like Jews. Still, she'd grown up with Jews, so it was normal to see them looking like themselves. This was during the period Mutti would get angry with her on an hourly basis for her asking where the Jews were going.

How should I know? Mutti would say. Now be quiet and…

But they have to go somewhere? Heike would insist.

I didn't say they weren't going anywhere, Mutti would reply, letting every ounce of exasperation enter her voice, I simply said I didn't know where they're going.

But how can they take them away, Heike would continue, if

they don't know where they're taking them? WHO SAID THEY DON'T KNOW WHERE THEY'RE TAKING THEM? Mutti would now begin to scream. ALL I SAID WAS, I DON'T KNOW WHERE THEY'RE TAKING THEM. IF YOU ASK ME ONE MORE TIME WHERE THEY'RE TAKING THEM, I'M GOING TO BRAIN YOU WITH A FRYING PAN. This was Mutti's standard exit line. Either she would then leave, or, depending on how bad it was, you would. Mutti always felt Heike was asking these questions simply to make her mad but Heike genuinely wanted to know where the Jews had disappeared to. Toward the end of the expulsions, after she gave up asking Mutti and it became clear from her distracted but clearly deliberate silences that Julia wasn't going to tell her, Heike toyed with the idea of going straight to the source and asking one of the Jews waiting in one of the lines that then dotted the city. After all, they must know. But whenever the opportunity to ask arose, something about the Jew, or the circumstances, or the SS, or the weather...always prevented her.

* * *

The route Heike had chosen led today from Julia's apartment across Uber Platz, to Gras Strasse, to Streichholzer Allee (nobody knew why it was named that), to Krone Strasse, then a sharp right, and home at last: Vielenstrasse. It was a familiar route. Streichholzer Allee had some of the oldest houses in the city. Mutti said it was a mews. All the houses were two story and all of them had elaborate scroll work on the front. Some sported carved figures over their gaily painted front doors. Even now, in the depths of the bombings, the front doors remained brightly colored.

Heike had enjoyed walking on the pavement but Streichholzer Allee was quite narrow and if a truck or tank decided to come down it, she would have had to leap out of the way in a hurry. So she stepped onto the sidewalk. In the old days, people would come from all parts of the City, and even from other parts of Europe, to see Streichholzer Allee. Now it was all but deserted. A solitary old man swept snow off the front of his sidewalk. He was wearing an old flannel shirt over his baggy, cord pants. He had a hump back and had to stop after each shovelful to rest.

Suddenly Heike felt uneasy. For a moment, she wondered if it was the old man, but he was still several houses away. Since Herr Gruber, she didn't completely trust old men. They looked harmless enough, but you couldn't know what was going on inside their heads. Frail as this one seemed, it would be a simple matter for him to snatch her and drag her into his house. After all, he was a male, and she wasn't even five feet tall yet. Four eleven and a half. Soon she'd be five feet. Mutti said she would be more than five feet, probably five six. This was almost too much to hope for. If she reached five six, she would be as tall as many of the boys.

This, however, was in the future. At the moment, she was smaller than the old man. Better to brave the street, which was currently empty, than the unknown in the form of the shovel holder. Humming to herself, Heike skipped off the sidewalk just as piece of pediment broke free one house up and fell with a huge crash onto the street where she would have been had she kept walking on it.

For a few seconds, Heike stood where she was, paralyzed by a combination of disbelief and fear. She was vaguely aware that the old man had dropped his shovel and was running toward her. Also, a door had opened and a woman appeared, holding up the bottom of her apron. Why would she do that? Heike wondered. Probably because she was cooking. Or cleaning. And her hands were dirty. That must have been it.

The old man was the first to reach her.

Are you all right, Fraulein? he asked, brushing at her coat.

Heike nodded. The front of her coat, she noticed, was covered with snow and small bits of debris.

Are you sure? Come with me. You have cut your head.

What? said Heike?

The old man took hold of her arm and, as several residents of Streichholzer Allee appeared in their doorways, guided Heike to his house, whose entrance, despite the cold, was wide open. Inside, a fire burned in the fireplace, and Heike soon found herself in a cheerful, sparklingly clean kitchen as the old man and several female neighbors fussed over her. They wiped her forehead with a clean cloth, washed it with warm water, and prepared to apply a bandage.

When Heike awoke two hours later, it was already dark.
Someone was sitting beside her. For a moment, Heike was
afraid it was the old man. But a woman's voice asked her if she
awake.

Heike nodded and inquired where she was.

You slept for a while, the woman said. You are at the home of
Herr and Frau Strauss. On Streicholzer Allee. Do you remember
your accident?

No, Heike said.

Ah, said the woman. Well, a cornice fell and some fragments
hit you in the head. It could have been worse if you hadn't
stepped onto the sidewalk just when you did.

Would I have died? Heike asked, feeling the question was
strange. If she had died, she wouldn't have been able to ask it.
Being able to ask it meant she could enjoy the woman's answer,
whether it was yes, or no.

I think so. Yes, the woman replied. We were very worried for
a moment.

Do I have a concussion? Heike asked. She had learned about
concussions from Hans. Hans said the object of throwing an
enemy in hand to hand combat was not just to break a limb
but to throw him quickly enough to make his brain bounce off
his skull in order to give him a concussion. Hans liked to give
scientific explanations for what the close combat arm of Hitler
Youth had taught him to do to an enemy, as he called them.

What about Jews? Heike had asked.

What? said Hans. What about them?

Can you give them concussions?

Of course, Hans said. The Jew is inherently weak. Why ask
such a stupid question, idiot?

Because you always say they are stupid and have no brains.
So how can you get a concussion if you have no brain?

Heike had only reminded Hans of this because she knew it
would make him angry. Any mention of Jews made Hans angry.
Before, neither she nor Hans had thought much about Jews. You
could go an entire week without a Jew crossing your mind. After,
you couldn't walk down the street without seeing one, either a

real one or a Jew on a poster. The real ones often looked like everyone else, except for the star sewn on their coats. The poster Jews had hooked noses and full lips and huge insect like eyes. They gave Heike the willies.

When she asked Mutti about this disparity, Mutti had gotten as mad as Hans. Quick to take advantage of this, Heike from then on would often come home from school, or Franz's, and pretend to want to have a heart to heart with her mother, especially if Heike was bored, or Mutti was too distracted to pay attention to her. For example, Heike would sit at the table, put her cheek in her palm, yawn, and ask Mutti why they couldn't get someone who could draw Jews the way they appeared in real life instead of with huge noses and lips that hung off their mouths like caterpillars. Mutti, already past her limit, said how should she know and went on to say that if it was that important to Heike, why didn't she start taking art lessons; then she could draw Jews. Another time, Mutti had forbidden Heike to go to Julia's after school, so Heike had followed Mutti from room to room asking if any of the Jews in their building had killed Christian babies or raped Aryans. This ended when Mutti cuffed her on her ear and said, if Heike kept bothering her like this, she would lock her in her room for twenty four hours. Heike had run into the living room, flung herself on the couch, and cried until Mutti came in and apologized. It was one of her greatest triumphs.

Not that she wasn't actually curious about the Jews. There were, or had been, a lot of them in school, and although she didn't socialize with them, most of them anyway. Still, they were polite and clean and talked like everyone else. More or less. Some of the boys in the Boy's School wore their hair funny and had tablecloths sticking out of the bottom of their jackets. But none of them, as far as she could tell, had horns, like Wilma-Anna Demeulemeister said they did. She said she'd felt them once. That was why Hebrews always wore hats, to conceal their horns.

What about the girls? Claudia Knipf had asked.

They have long hair so they don't need hats, Wilma-Anna replied.

So, if I go up to a Jewish girl and touch her head, I will feel horns, Claudia said.

111

Yes, said Wilma-Anna, if she's a real Jew.

What does that mean? Julia had asked.

That's how you can tell, Wilma-Anna said, and there the discussion ended as the teacher, Fraulein Purtzfennig, came into the room.

Then of course, there was the shelter problem. In the early days, when everyone in the building went down to the shelter, (this was before Heike made it her business to be there first), the building's Jews had gone too. Heike could remember numerous times when she sat with, or across from, Amelia Rosenfeld, who was two years older than she was, but small for her age. After a while, she and Amelia would play hand games, like patty cake, which both agreed were stupid but which passed the time while they were waiting for the bombers to come so they could see whether or not they would live. Amelia said she was certain the bombers wouldn't destroy their building, but when Heike pressed her, she could never give a good reason why. So far, she had been right, even though, two or three months later, or perhaps four, she was no longer there to enjoy the fruits of her prediction.

This had been one of the reasons Heike resisted the move to the Rosenfeld apartment. She felt she would be being disloyal to Amelia. Of course, she told no one. Hans would have used it against her, and Mutti, who was much more sensitive than Hans, but who wasn't? would have sat her down and said she was being unreasonable, and that Amelia would have liked her, Heike, to have her old room, and that if they didn't take it, the SS and Frau Brest would want to know why, which might make trouble for the family. Whichever tack Mutti took, Heike would have felt at a disadvantage. So she eventually gave in and said, okay, she would move.

Now, she rarely thought about Amelia, although she still thought about Jews. You couldn't help it. They were always bringing them up in school. For example, Fraulein Purtzfennig, the same one whose appearance had broken up the discussion about Jew's horns, gave a once a week lecture on the Jewish menace: how the true danger of the Jew was the way he had taken on the protective coloration of the Aryan, so that, unless you were sensitive to their smell, or had made an extensive study of their body language and hand gestures, they might fool you into thinking they were normal. Everyone except for the dullest, least pretty girls tried to doze off during these lectures. For one thing, there were no longer any Jews to be afraid of. And for another, a lot of the more popular and prettier girls agreed among themselves that Jews didn't smell that different from Aryans, and some, the richer ones, actually smelled better. They giggled during this discussion, knowing that they were participating in something that was actually dangerous and could get them in serious trouble if someone reported them.

No one had. Not yet, anyway. Now, Fraulein Purtzfennig said, the Jews that the Fuhrer hadn't been able to round up had fled to England and were using the money they'd stolen from hard working Aryans to finance the British bombings. This was what gave the issue so much urgency: just when you thought you had solved the entire problem, it cropped up someplace else with even more virulence than before. Here Hanna Gemeinhardt, Heike's friend and the second brightest girl in the class, had raised her hand asked what virulence meant, even though she knew full well what it meant and Fraulein Purtzfennig knew she knew, but she couldn't do anything about it because Hanna always looked serious and never gave away that she might be mocking you. The best thing was just to answer her question, so Fraulein Purtzfennig said "Disease carrying" and continued with her lesson.

Heike blinked. The woman had asked her something which she hadn't registered. She thought she'd heard the word concussion, but perhaps she'd made it up, so she waited until the woman spoke again.

Do you have a headache, dear? the woman asked.

Heike did have a headache, but not a bad one. Plus, she felt very weak. And very tired. Not tired the way she usually did, after a boring day of school, and an after-school session of physical fitness where you had to run around a track a hundred times shouting patriotic slogans, at least it seemed like a hundred times. More like the tired you got when there hadn't been enough to eat for a few days and you didn't want to get out of bed. You just wanted to curl up under the covers and let sleep take you back after you luxuriated in the way cold air felt on your face for a few seconds before burying it re-under the comforter.

Heike nodded, which hurt, and said, Yes, she did have a

headache, but a small one, not a very big one.

The woman too nodded and said, This is why we want you to stay with us for bit. To make certain you are all right. As soon as the bombing is over, we will send someone to inform your family that you are all right.

There's just my mother, Heike said. I should go back to her.

Yes, the woman said, very gently, but you see, the curfew will begin in an hour, and I'm afraid you won't be ready to go home before that. They are expecting a heavy air raid tonight so everyone must be in the shelter by six o'clock. .

What time is it now? asked Heike, alarmed.

Five, said the woman.

I have to go, Heike said, pushing the covers away. Mutti will be worried about me. Especially with Hans gone. I have to...

Where do you live, child? the woman asked, putting a hand on Heike's shoulder and gently easing her back into the immensely comfortable bed. Heike felt dizzy and a little nauseous, and didn't resist.

Vielenstrasse, 118, Heike said aloud. At least, she said to herself, I think that's it. There was no doubt she lived on Vielenstrasse but, for some reason, she didn't feel as confident about the number. The exact apartment number, for the moment, eluded her.

Our name is Meitner, Heike added, feeling on firmer ground here. Mine is Heike and my mother's is Trudi.

I see, the woman said. Good. I am Frau Strauss. Let me go and see if Herbert, that is my husband, can tell your mother you are all right. Vielenstrasse is quite close, after all.

Frau Strauss got to her feet, smiled at Heike, and left the room.

Heike closed her eyes. To her knowledge, this was the first time she had ever slept in a strange bed. Julia's didn't count. She'd known Julia since they were little girls and she had stayed at her apartment numerous times. When they were little, she and Julia even slept in the same bed, a large double bed made of dark wood with a white canopy floating overhead. They would be sleeping in the same bed today if it was up to them, but Julia's mother said that it was time they slept in separate beds and would order the family's servants, they had three, to move a portable bed into Julia's room whenever Heike stayed over.

The portable bed was lumpy and had a gully down the middle, unlike this bed, which was the most comfortable bed Heike had ever lain on and felt like a cloud of whipped cream. The room, a garret room, was also comfortable, nicely furnished from what Heike could see, with landscape paintings on the walls. The paintings were of meadows with mountains in the background. One meadow had cows on it, and another had bales of hay.

It seemed impossible that anyone could die in this room, that's how comfortable and cozy it was. There were rooms where Heike had felt you could die. The pantry in their apartment was one such room. Heike hated to go into it and often ignored Mutti, or pretended she hadn't heard her, when Mutti asked Heike to get something from it, usually a can of food, or some paper. If you just looked at the pantry, you wouldn't see anything strange about it. But Heike felt the room was possessed and avoided it like the plague, even at the risk of really displeasing Mutti, as opposed to baiting her.

After a while, Frau Strauss returned, bringing Herr Strauss with her. Heike felt uncomfortable at a strange man being in the room, even though it was his house. But he was old and seemed kind and soon she began to relax. Herr Strauss asked her again where she lived, and if her mother would be home. Heike told him and said, Yes, she was certain she'd be there.

Herr Strauss nodded and said, in that case, he would put on his boots and overcoat and walk over to tell Frau Meitner her daughter was perfectly safe. If Frau Meitner liked, she could come back with him and spend the night at their house with Heike. There was plenty of room, and, if the two of them preferred, they could bring up a second bed and her mother could sleep here.

Heike thanked him and suddenly began to cry. She wasn't certain why she was crying. Maybe because of the concussion. But maybe too because of everything. Even though she'd wanted Hans to leave, and had been happy that he was gone and she no longer had to fight with him for the bathroom, or listen to him go on about the Fuhrer, or the Jews, or catch a glimpse of him looking at himself in the mirror in his Hitler Youth uniform, she missed him. His absence made their apartment seem large and vacant. She hadn't felt this way about their father, about whom she rarely thought. When he left, everything immediately felt better. This should have been the case with Hans, but, for some reason, it wasn't.

Another reason she might have been crying, Heike thought, was the visit to Julia. Much as she loved Julia, and loved going there and seeing their apartment, with the grand piano, and the art, and the decorations and the plush, dark maroon furniture, and the photographs of Julia's father with the Fuhrer and the Reichfuhrer and other notables, today's visit had disconcerted her. It was as if a transparent curtain had come down and now separated her from her friend. This was probably not at all the case. Just because Julia had lost her virginity and she hadn't was no reason they couldn't continue to be as close as they'd always been. And yet, Heike wondered if this was true. Could a non-virgin really maintain a soul bond with a virgin? And if not, did that mean she too had to lose her virginity, if for no other reason than to preserve their friendship?

Finally, there was the question of Death. What would happen if she died tonight? She wouldn't have had a chance to make up her mind about whether it was worth the horror of letting a boy do what he had to do to you in order to take your virginity just so she could remain friends with her best friend. This was not to say it wasn't worth it. Just that it was a decision that would take time. And if she was killed, she wouldn't have the time to make it, or do anything else for that matter.

This, Heike felt as she began to drift off, was the conundrum of thinking about Death. To think about it, you had to be alive. But what you were thinking about was a State in which you couldn't think about anything. So you were thinking of a time when you couldn't think, but when you couldn't think, you wouldn't be able to think you wouldn't be able to think. These thoughts made her head spin. Surely things were simpler than this.

And yet, they weren't. Someone was going to bomb them tonight, but she hadn't done anything to deserve it. At least, she was pretty certain she hadn't. Hans might have. At least he might have wanted to. But so far, unless he had gotten to the Front already, he probably hadn't. Mutti hadn't either, to her knowledge. There may have been times Heike felt Mutti deserved to be bombed. But these were because Mutti had behaved irrationally or unfairly, not because she had done something wrong politically. The neighbor may have deserved a good bombing. Frau Brest certainly did. Herr Gruber she felt mixed about. She liked having company when she ran downstairs and was first in the shelter, but she didn't like the way he was always touching her. Yet, if she was to lose her virginity, she would have to undress in front of a boy. The thought made her shudder. Worse, he would need to undress in front of her. Not Herr Gruber, of course. It probably took him all day to get into his pajamas, he was so old.

Heike giggled. The thought of Herr Gruber trying to put an old bony leg through a pajama bottom was so funny she would have laughed out loud if she wasn't so exhausted. As it was, a giggle cost her a lot of energy. It was worth it. In Heike's version, Herr Gruber missed the pajama leg, and went hopping around the room on one foot until he fell. He lay there on his back, like a praying mantis, trying to free his leg. Poor Herr Gruber. Heike didn't like his jokes. She didn't like the way he always wore the armband. Even to the shelter. She didn't like the way he touched her. But she felt sorry for him all the same.

IV: THE LAST SUPPER

.1.

During the night, Trudi was awakened twice by dreams. All she remembered was a path leading up the side of an excavated hill. This made no sense, but left her feeling dread. When she finally woke for good, at 7am, it was snowing, and she felt the relief all Berliners felt when it snowed. Snow meant no air raids. It meant a quiet day, and, much more, a quiet night.

There was hot water, Trudi discovered on entering the bathroom, and she took a quick shower. Soaping her breasts, she thought briefly about Rolph and what to do about him. In the clear light of day, it was inconceivable she would report him to the SS. He was her lover. Had been her lover at any rate. She was undecided whether to allow him to remain so. Setting aside the danger to her, there was the risk her association with a possible Jew posed for the children. Heike was too young to come under suspicion but Hans might be ruined if it got out her mother had associated with a Hebrew.

After she dressed, Trudi sat at the kitchen table and composed, as she always did, a list of what she needed to do that day. She needed to wake Heike and make her breakfast, see to it she dressed warmly for her visit to Julia, (about which Trudi felt ambivalent but not ambivalent enough to make a fuss over it). She then needed to put away last night's dry dishes, set the few remaining potatoes in cold water so that they would freshen and expand, take her last remaining brooch out of its case in the event she found someone selling meat, and go out and hunt food for the family supper.

Done with the list, which she wrote in neat, block letters, Trudi rose and strode into Heike's bedroom. Heike was asleep on her side, mouth open, her face mashed into the pillow. She looked five years old. Suddenly flush with love, Trudi sat beside her daughter and gently shook her shoulder. It was amazing to Trudi how much she could still love this child, who irritated her so much in the course of an average day.

Trudi shook her again and Heike moaned, opened her eyes,

said What? and closed them again.

It's time to get up, Trudi said. If you're going to Julia's.

What time is it? Heike asked.

Eight, said Trudi.

Let Hans go first, said Heike.

Trudi bit her lower lip. Hans has left, remember? she said, suddenly understanding the source of her earlier dread. She was worried about him. His train had probably crossed the border by now. He was in Poland, with the other Hitler Youth, and had either stopped there, or was going on to the Ukraine, where pivotal battles were now being fought. Though there was nothing she could do about it, and though, being practical, she understood worry would get her nowhere, Trudi couldn't help herself. She worried about Hans with all her heart and only by exerting all her will did she prevent herself from crying out.

Oh, Heike said. Good. With this, she sat up, yawned, and reached over to allow her mother to hug her. Trudi took her daughter into her arms and kissed her musty hair. Go take a shower, she said. Go. While there's still hot water.

Back in the kitchen, Trudi made herself a cup of ersatz tea and sat by the window, drinking it. Snowflakes swirled down the air shaft in ever thicker spirals, almost obscuring the yellowish brick of the opposite wall. Snow. She'd loved snow ever since she was a child. Some winters, she almost went mad with frustration as day after day passed without the first snowfall. Then, suddenly, it would happen. She'd wake and either the sky was dark gray and snow was coming. Or the world was white, because snow had come while she was asleep. Either way. Either way she would take it.

By the time Heike arrived for breakfast, Trudi had crossed the first item off the list, washed her tea cup, and made a small bowl of oatmeal from something which, they all joked, might or might not have actually grown on a plant. They were perpetually hungry now. Even those of them who worked in party positions, or for the authorities, went to sleep hungry. There simply wasn't enough food to go around. Of course, their sacrifice was nothing when compared with what the men were going through. Still, her stomach ached sometimes with hunger.

You know what, Mutti? Heike said as she sat down at the table and picked up her spoon.

No. Tell me, Trudi said.

I thought I was going to be happy Hans was gone, but I miss him.

I do too, Trudi said.

That's different, Heike said. He's your son. He's just my brother.

Trudi smiled.

I used to love him when he was little, Heike continued. Mutti. Why do boys change? You know, when they start to have pimples?

Trudi laughed. The words Eat your oatmeal sprang to her mouth, as some variant of them always did when Heike asked her impossible questions. Today, however, Trudi felt she should answer her. But how? To tell the truth, even she didn't completely understand what happened to males once they reached puberty. One day they were sweet, innocent, loving; the next, while they were still innocent, they were angry, hostile, impossible.

It's hormones, Trudi said. Before they reach…thirteen…they don't have hormones. Not the same ones at any rate. Once they become teenagers, hormones…intrude on their bodies and make them aggressive and irrational. But this passes.

When?, Heike asked, spooning the thin gruel into her mouth.

When they reach twenty, Trudi said, hoping this would put an end to the discussion.

Heike thought about it a moment, then said, Then what?

What do you mean, Then what? Trudi asked, feeling the familiar irritation rising into her chest.

You know. What do they do then? Heike asked.

What do you mean, What do they do then? What do they do now? Trudi replied, doing her best to stifle the irritation, but failing.

Heike was silent a moment, obliviously contemplating her oatmeal. Why do they have to want to have sex? she said after a moment.

Trudi was about to start yelling, but from somewhere managed to summon sufficient reserves to stop herself. The kitchen, though cold, suddenly felt quite warm. Trudi glanced out the fogged-up window and saw nothing. Not snow, not not snow. Just condensate. Another miracle of chemistry, she said to herself, like solid objects falling out of the sky, hitting the ground, and fracturing into a thousand pieces. Chemistry. That's what we are. The end result of chemistry.

I don't want to talk about this now, Trudi said. What I do want to talk about is your putting on galoshes and a scarf before you go out. And don't say you don't need galoshes, because if you don't need galoshes, you don't need to visit Julia. I'm tired of having to have this fight with you every day. Today of all days, I want you to listen to me.

Why Today of all days, Heike asked.

Because I'm worried sick about Hans, Trudi shouted, losing it, as they both knew she would. Because my eldest child has been sent to the war and may never return. And because you're thirteen and I want you to act thirteen instead of acting like a five year old who needs her mother to button her coat and make her put on appropriate clothing.

Again Heike was silent for a moment, as if thinking this over. Then she said, Okay, Mutti. I'll wear galoshes.

* * *

Once Heike had left, and this item had been crossed off the list, Trudi stowed her tea cup, ate the little porridge which remained in the pot, rinsed the pot and poured the first rinse into a second tea cup from which she drank it. Someone was knocking on her front door. Herr Gruber probably. He often knocked on his way downstairs to ask if there was anything he could get them. Yes, thought Trudi, you can get me a nice big roast beef with potatoes and cabbage and a bottle or two of wine. Oh, and you can bring General Jodl back with you so Jodl and I can discuss arranging Hans's prompt return. And while you're at it, why not bring me a carton of cigarettes and the assurance that Alfred won't come back from the war.

It was in this mood she opened the door to find Rolph standing there, a newspaper wrapped package under his arm.

Am I disturbing you, he asked.

No, she lied. Come in.

Rolph stepped into the entryway and stood a moment, holding the package in one hand, his hat in the other. The package, Trudi noticed, had begun to seep a red liquid and she wondered what it could be.

I wanted to apologize for yesterday, Rolph began. It was wrong of me to tell you about my...problem.

Trudi nodded, impassive, her gaze fixed on the leaking package.

I wasn't thinking clearly, Rolph continued. After you left, I sat down and considered the matter from your point of view. Of course you wouldn't want to know about this problem. You can't possibly help me with it and, if they do find out, my having told you...All I can say is, I will never tell them about our conversation.

Do you have any more news? Trudi asked, as she pointed to the package and added, What's that?

What? Oh, said Rolph. Half a shoulder round. Klaus Faust gave it to me yesterday. His sister...

Half a what? Trudi asked, thinking she had heard him incorrectly.

Shoulder roast, Rolph repeated. Klaus's sister has a farm in Hanover. She came in yesterday with some beef and he gave me this as thanks for helping him with an algorithm.

Oh, Trudi said, momentarily unable to take it in. What had he brought it down here for, she wondered. To torment me? To let it drip on her floor and add another item to my list? Why? The very fact of his having it here, in her apartment, was surreal enough.

No, Rolph was saying, no more news. There won't be until I receive the last of great grandfather's papers from Schwabia. Until then, I've decided not to worry, he continued, handing her the meat, which she now saw was wrapped in old issues of Beobachter Zeitung.

Why are you giving this to me? Trudi asked, uncomprehending.

So you can make it. I won't have time. There'll be a large air raid tonight, they think, and I'll be busy with that from the moment I come home from work. Would you mind? I thought you could cook it and you, Heike, and perhaps I, can have it for supper before we go to the shelter.

You want me to cook it, Trudi said.

Are you all right, Trudi? asked Rolph.

Trudi nodded. Shocked, is all.

Well, it will put all of us in a better frame of mind, Rolph said. With any luck, Hans will be back in time to have some.

Trudi blinked and stared at Rolph. His long, fine featured face appeared completely serious; but how could it be, given what he had just said to her?

What are you talking about, Rolph? she asked, her voice quivering with rage.

Oh. You probably haven't heard. They've recalled trains from all over Germany. Including the train that took Hans to Liebenswald.

Liebenswald? Trudi repeated.

Normally, they stay there an entire week, but I understand they were on their way back as of last night. It must be serious if Himmler allowed them to break things off without...without achieving the maximum number of couplings. Insane as that is. Insane. Insane. Insane.

Oblivious now to the roast beef, which was leaking onto her hands, Trudi sat and tried to make sense of what Rolph was saying. One of them, she felt, had gone mad. Perhaps it was she herself, but more likely, news that he might be a Jew had made Rolph insane. In any case, he was making no sense.

As if intuiting how Trudi felt, Rolph walked over and put a hand on her shoulder. I have to go, he said. Maybe I should have just let him surprise you. But I'm fairly certain he'll be back tonight, tomorrow morning at the latest. I'm not sure if this will be good news or bad...

Lebensborn?, Trudi whispered. You're joking with me.

...since, Rolph continued, it probably means they're about to send Hitler Youth to the front. But at least he'll be with you while he waits to be assigned.

Lebensborn, Trudi said again and, in spite of herself, began to laugh. Rolph stared at her, and it gradually dawned on him that only now did she actually know where her son had been.

.2.

After Trudi released Rolph, having convinced herself what he'd just told her was true, she boned, cubed, and marinated the roast beef in a bit of wine; then, letting it sit, she put on her warmest clothes and walked to the nearest tram stop to catch a tram to the train station. Because the snow was still thick, the tram was almost on top of them before those waiting to board could see it. When they did, it looked, with its cap of snow, like a toy.

Inside the tram, Trudi unbuttoned her coat and took a seat beside a large, placid woman, whose gloved hands lay atop one another. Neither she nor the woman spoke. This was fine with Trudi, who needed time to compose herself. Hans hated it when she became emotional, and especially hated it whenever she was demonstrative in public. He called this Jewish behavior, and asked, rhetorically, what good was it to rid the country of Jews if Aryans were going to behave like them?

At Krenze Strasse, the tram halted to allow a tank convoy to pass. Trudi could feel their vibrations in her womb. She wanted to rub the condensate off their window so she could see the tanks, but the placid woman remained facing front and Trudi felt shy of leaning across and perhaps bothering her.

At last, the tanks cleared and the tram made the rest of the journey unobstructed, though it slowed now and then for work gangs clearing rubble from yesterday's bombings. It was common knowledge these gangs were comprised of prisoners of war, though their exact racial makeup was unclear. Trudi assumed most were Russian. Soon, if Rolph was correct, Hans would be facing men like them, only better fed of course and armed. Trudi had no doubt the Germans would defeat people who looked like this, yet there were hordes of them, too numerous to count. We could eliminate hundreds, thousands, and there would be thousands more.

* * *

The apron in front of the Bahnhof was packed with women and there was nothing for Trudi to do but join them and let their forward momentum carry her inside. Most of the women were her age or a little younger. All were dressed in their warmest clothing. The majority were of a lower social class. Their clothes, unlike hers, came from cheap department stores and showed considerable signs of wear. Trudi searched their anxious faces for one she knew, but recognized no one.

After several minutes, the incessant pressure building behind her popped Trudi through the Bahnhof doors and into a lobby as crowded with women as the apron outside. Here however, people scurried this way and that in unceasing but illegible patterns. Every so often, a woman would stop and the crowds would part and flow around her, as if she were rock in a stream. Trudi herself was about to stop when she recognized Frau Prusseldorf, whom she had met a Hitler Youth parent function,

Hello Frau Prusseldorf, Trudi said. Do you remember me? I'm Hans Meitner's mother.

Frau Prusseldorf blinked, then nodded. Of course. I have been here an hour now.

Yes, Trudi said. It's madness.

I finally told someone I would have him arrested if he didn't give me the number of the platform our sons are arriving on. You have to be firm with them or you will get nowhere.

Exactly, Trudi agreed, not liking the woman. What is the track number, Frau Prusseldorf.

18. I went to the bathroom as I understood the train was not expected for twenty minutes. Yet I had to wait twelve minutes for a toilet. You should have seen the toilet. A horse wouldn't use it.

Now all I want, Frau Prusseldorf continued, is to collect Carl and take him home. Our maid has made schnitzel for him. It's his favorite. She makes it in the Bavarian fashion, even though she's not from Bavaria.

Yes, I'm sure he'll like it, Trudi said, spotting the entrance to track 18 which, like the other entrances, was packed with women. Here we are. I think I will go on ahead.

The train will be late in any case, Frau Prusseldorf said, keeping to Trudi's side. She wore a fur coat with a fox collar and a thick cloche which covered her ears. Her wide mouth was thin and heavily made up with red lipstick that extended over the rims of her lips. Her eyes were purple and never stood still. It used to be you could set your clock by the arrival and departure of our trains. That was before they began using trains to take them away. Not that I object to that, except at moments like this when I want to see my child. Can you believe the children will return having lost their virginity, she asked as she pushed her way toward the edge of the concrete platform. A freezing wind blew down the track, at the far end of which was gray daylight.

Trudi stopped listening. Frau Prusseldorf had bulldozed clear a small section of platform and Trudi took advantage of this to claim a spot from which she could look directly into the windows of an approaching train. To her surprise, Trudi was conscious of a feeling of rising excitement, similar to that she felt as a young woman when she was about meet a boyfriend. This was silly, she told herself. Hans has only been gone two days. Why are you so eager to see him?

When Trudi looked to her left , Frau Prusseldorf was gone. In her place were two enormous women, both wearing mink coats. Sisters, she believed. Trudi edged away from them. She wanted to be as solitary as possible. She wanted to concentrate on greeting Hans and not annoying him with a display of emotion. She would say, should say, something like Hello Hans, Let's get home quickly as I still have to cook. Or, Hans, do you mind leading the way? The crowding is completely insane. No. Not insane. Impossible. Yes. It's impossible to move in here.

A whistle sounded and a murmur ran through the crowd. A train was approaching. Women pushed toward the front of the platform and Trudi had to dig her heels in to keep from being pushed too close to the edge. For a moment, she feared she might fall. But the train, visible now, was arriving on a track two over from theirs. The commotion that had almost endangered her subsided and Trudi was able to move back a bit, so that if the crowd again pushed forward when their train did arrive, she would be safe.

* * *

An hour later a cry went up at the front of their platform. Their train had arrived. This time, movement on the platform was lateral, not vertical, and Trudi and the other women were pushed toward the track's opening where the locomotive was visible, expelling a steady funnel of white smoke, Trudi's heart was beating wildly. Her son was on that train. Her only son.

* * *

When the train finally came to a stop, the first off were SS, who cleared a path through the women with their usual efficiency. Once the path was established, they stood with their backs to the crowd, staring back at the empty entrances.

Is this the train from Liebenswald?, Trudi asked an SS. He stared at her blankly, then walked away,

Yes, Liebenswald, a woman said. Trudi thanked her.

Surrounded now on all sides, Trudi was finding it hard to breathe. Though the train was stationary, its engine continued to idle, beating a steady thrum into the chests of the onlookers. An eternity passed, and then a few Hitler Youth appeared and began to descend the train's steps to the platform. They looked exhausted. They also looked unfamiliar. Trudi tried to move toward the front, but it was like moving through solid ice.

Trudi waited, listening for the sounds of reunions which were certain to be taking place. She heard none. As she was about to ask her neighbor what was happening, a woman at the front of the crowd said these were boys from Essen, not Berlin. They had been put on this train because the train from Berlin had been re-routed.

Re-routed where, women began to cry out, as the news spread along the platform. Re-routed why? Here and there the questions were punctuated with shouts or cries of anguish. The SS began to bark orders at the women, whom the boys, moving in a somnolence just shy of slow motion, completely ignored. They seemed stunned.

A boy Trudi thought she recognized appeared, not from Essen, from Berlin. Trudi pushed forward and called to him.

Hello. Hello, she waved. Are you from Liebenswald? Do you know Hans Meitner?

The boy turned to look at her.

I'm his mother, Trudi said. Hans Meitner. He's in the Vielenstrasse Brigade.

The boy turned away without breaking stride.

You are from Liebenswald, yes?, Trudi called after him. You were there for Lebensborn,

Hush, several voices admonished her. The SS nearest Trudi began to stride over and some women hustled Trudi into their midst, walling her off so the SS couldn't find her.

On the platform, the parade of Hitler Youth had thinned to a trickle. A few stragglers brought up the rear, looking like boys who had stayed up too long after bedtime. There were deep circles under their eyes and they moved lethargically, as though not fully awake.

Like the other women, Trudi continued to scan their faces, her gaze bouncing from one to another, then back again, then from one to the other. But she was certain now that none of them would be Hans.

.3.

Rolph had been going up and down stairs all day. First, he walked the half mile to Reinhold Shlager's offices where he was informed that the weather was expected to clear by 2 pm and allied bombers would arrive on schedule. Through intermediaries, Shlager ordered all air wardens to instruct residents to write their next of kin on their forearms, in ink. As a further precaution, children were to be given name tags to wear around their necks in case they became separated from their parents.

Rolph received his orders in dutiful silence, descended three flights of ministry stairs, walked back to his apartment building through clearing skies, ascended five flights of stairs to his apartment, changed out of his wet socks, then went downstairs to the basement bomb shelter to make sure there was sufficient food and water to keep everyone supplied for three days. Rolph's assistant, Manfred Winkle, was already there, stacking large metal cans of water. Winkle told Rolph he thought there was enough water for two days. He'd heard through the grapevine however that 118 Glotz Strasse had stored enough for five days. Perhaps Rolph could ask if they could borrow a day's worth.

Rolph said he would, then spent a fruitless half hour traversing the stairs of 118 Glotz looking for its air-raid warden, finally leaving a message with a desiccated old woman who had watched his ascents and descents from behind her chained front door. When he finally arrived back at Trudi's apartment, in the late afternoon, after again changing his socks since his boots had a hole in them, he felt exhausted.

Trudi answered his knock immediately and let him in. The smell of roasting meat filled Rolph's nostrils and he suddenly felt faint with hunger. Trudi waved him away from the door so she could replace the dish towels preventing the meat's aroma from escaping under the door into the building proper. It was considered impolite to advertise one's cooking when, on some days, some residents of the building might eat nothing.

I came to tell you I won't be able to eat with you tonight, Rolph said, noting that Trudi looked tired and vulnerable.

Why not? she asked.

I have to find more water, then make certain the auxiliary batteries are working in case we lose electricity. Which appears likely, since we usually do. Then I have to make certain the men who keep the census have pens so that, if possible, they can have everyone entering the shelter write their next of kin on their arms. No one seems to have thought that, if they're killed by bombs, it's unlikely the writing will remain, never mind the next of kin.

There is no ink, Trudi reminded him. There hasn't been for a year.

Rolph smiled dryly. You're harping on details, he said.

Both of them smiled.

I'll save you some roast, Trudi said, feeling a pang of regret that he wouldn't be able to eat with them.

Did you find Hans? Rolph asked.

How do you know...? Trudi began

Herr Gruber saw you leave for the station. He told me. He's taken to looking out his window for hours at a time, now that Heike ignores him.

Again they smiled at one another. Rolph turned toward the door.

Here, let me give you something to eat, Trudi said, knowing full well there was nothing she could give him beside the roast, which was not yet done.

Yes? Rolph asked.

Let me see.

Trudi opened a food drawer and they both peered in. At the bottom was a bottle containing a half inch of jam.

I'll put this on a piece of bread. There's a piece left, Trudi said.

That's all right. I'll have something downstairs, Rolph said, studying at her more closely. She looked, underneath her perpetual coolness, a coolness that never failed to attract him, frantic.

No, Trudi said. Eat here. Wait. I don't want you to go yet.

Rolph raised his eyebrows. This was unlike her and he asked if she was okay.

I'm fine, Trudi said. But I want you to fuck me.

What? Rolph asked, as startled by her talking this way as he was by the timing.

Yes. I know. We can do it quickly, Trudi said, without apologizing.

I told Manfred I'd be back in five minutes, Rolph said.

Manfred is a grown man, Trudi said, as though this were a debate in which each must counter the other's argument.

Yes, Rolph conceded. But there are things…

We'll be done before you know he knows you're gone, Trudi continued, as if they were talking about doing the dishes.

What about Heike? Rolph asked, feeling his penis stir.

She's at Julia's. She won't be back for an hour.

Where do we do it?

Here, Trudi said, lifting her skirt and beginning to lower her thick wool stockings.

Here, Rolph said.

I'm already wet, said Trudi, her breath coming fast.

This isn't like you, said Rolph, undoing his belt.

Trudi nodded and pulled down her underpants. Rolph reached down. She was soaking wet and his penis rose to its full height. He levered it free of his undershorts and began to maneuver for position so that he could guide it into her.

Here. Let me help, Trudi said.

Rolph felt her fingers grip the shaft. He leaned in as she guided the tip toward her vagina, and bit her softly on the neck.

I like that. That's nice, Trudi said. Bite again. Harder.

It will leave a mark.

Harder, she demanded pushing her sweater up to expose her brassiere.

Rolph bit again, feeling his erection slide into her vulva. Trudi gasped and Rolph bit her ear, then eased them both to the wall so that she could brace herself while he undid her bra and cupped her breasts. Both of them expelled harsh guttural breaths.

Trudi moaned as Rolph began to move in her. Faster, she commanded. Do it faster.

Rolph complied, reaching down and gripping her thigh with his left hand. It quivered and he released the thick upper muscle so that he could run his finger up toward the base of her anus. Trudi gasped and said Yes.

Fuck me, she said.

Yes, oh yes. Don't say that or I'll…

Fuck me, fuck me, Trudi repeated, her hands flat against the wall, her head drooping toward her chest so that her hair fell on either side of her cheeks. Rolph could see her face, the skin blotched, her eyes tightly shut. She looked unfinished-- hermetic and wild. Rolph wanted to bite her so hard the bites would leave marks. He took the nape of her thin neck in his mouth and held it there.

Trudi said Yes, and grew soft, almost limp. Rolph pushed against her so hard that her hips hit the wall and she staggered a bit, compelling him to catch her. She laughed and, for a second, Rolph was afraid he would come. But he stopped moving in time and both regained their balance.

I'm going to come, Trudi said, talking to herself. I'm going to come. Don't let me scream. Oh God, give me something to bite. Give me something to bite. Bite my lip, she commanded.

Rolph put the blade of his hand between her teeth.

I'm going to come, Trudi cried in a strangled voice. Oh God. I'm going to come.

Rolph pushed her head down further so that it's crown butted the wall. Trudi began to cry out, softly at first, then louder. Rolph pushed his hand deeper into her mouth and felt his own orgasm rise up from below his stomach.

Trudi was screaming now, silently. Rolph couldn't see her eyes but knew they open and unseeing. She was seeing nothing, as he was seeing nothing. Whatever was happening felt like it might extinguish him. He too wanted to shout but suppressed it, exclaiming instead in guttural syllables that meant nothing,

Trudi too made noises-- high pitched and primitive. Rolph thought he could make out the word Jew, repeated over and over until it became a long, guttural cry, ending only when her orgasm ended and Trudi sagged, limp and sweating, her face pressed against the wall.

Rolph, who had also come, let his entire weight press against Trudi and he remained like that a moment, waiting for his breathing to calm down. When his mind began to settle, he felt the desire to ask her why she'd been saying the word Jew, but he decided against it. She had said it was all. She herself probably didn't know why, except that, at the moment, for whatever reason, it added to her pleasure. That was what the act was about, intense pleasure subsiding into quiet, perhaps sometimes mixed with a measure of disquiet, or, if one was lucky, a measure of love.

I have to go, Rolph said when, after a moment, both of them began to stir.

It's okay, Trudi said in her normal tone of voice and moved so that he could ease himself out of her.

That was nice, Trudi said.

Rolph zipped up his pants. Can I use the bathroom first, he asked.

Trudi nodded, stepping out of her underpants and lowering her skirt. Her sweater still rose to her armpits and Rolph could see her breasts, their nipples pink and swollen. He cinched his belt and cupped a breast, testing its weight. Then he kissed it, taking the nipple into his mouth, savoring its fleshy taste. It stiffened and, incredibly, he felt himself begin to grow hard.

* * *

In the bathroom, Rolph washed his crotch, then his hands, then his face. He dried himself, straightened his tie, put his jacket back on, and looked at himself in the mirror. He had always thought of sex as a way for people to bridge distance so it made sense that Trudi called him a Jew, or called something a Jew. Just as it made sense he wanted her immediately after he'd had her, because he hadn't had her. He couldn't. One couldn't. There was something in her one couldn't have, no matter what one did. So he could never fully have her. But paradoxically, this gave him renewed opportunity to try. To try and try again. It had, even before he became a Jew.

* * *

With Rolph out of the kitchen, Trudi leaned her back against the wall and wondered what had just happened. Not to them, but to her. She'd never behaved like this before, never allowed herself to speak like this to a lover. Certainly not to her husband, to whom she would never have said such things, even if he'd permitted her to talk during their brief, brutal sex. So the way she had spoken must have had something to do with Rolph. With his prospective Jewishness. With certain as yet unknown things that had already taken root in her psyche. Trudi wasn't certain she wanted to know what these were, not now anyway. The sensations and emotions that had wracked her were not yet completely settled. She was still under their spell, as surely as Rolph's come was trickling down her thigh, though the latter was merely physical.

Trudi picked her underpants off the floor and used them to wipe up the semen. She drank a glass of water and sat at the kitchen table. Sunlight was pouring through the window. The storm had broken. They would be bombed after all.

Yet this had no significance for her, not just yet. She felt she had already been bombed, bombed by something she barely understood. Love? This seemed unlikely. She liked and respected and admired and felt contempt and impatience for Rolph. She wanted him and at times, though not now, hated herself for wanting him. She would have to wait and see.

She didn't have to wait long. Rolph emerged from the bathroom neatly dressed and, except for a slight flush, looking as if he had just stopped in to drop something off and was ready to leave again. Trudi studied his face for a sign, though she wasn't sure of what. Love? He looked as he always did: affectionate, warm, wry, faintly wary, but frank and curious. These were just words. He looked like himself, Trudi thought.

Instead of leaving, Rolph sat beside her, took her hand, kissed it, then reached under her skirt and placed his palm flat on her sex, despite the fact it was soaking wet from both of them. He kept it there a moment, staring into her eyes, then kissed her lightly, got up, washed his hands, and said he would try to make it for dinner. If not, he would see her in the shelter. Afterwards, they could talk. He wanted to talk. But now was not the time, or, rather, now there wasn't time. He kissed her again and left.

Trudi continued to sit in the kitchen a moment, aware once more of the rich smell of cooking meat, which in its own way was also almost too much to bear. She rose and lifted the lid off the pot. The meat had turned brown and the vegetables had browned at the edges. Underneath, what remained of the wine had mixed with the cooking fat and was gently bubbling away.

.4.

When Heike woke, it was already dark. She could hear the wind batting against shutters and was puzzled. They didn't have shutters. Then she remembered. Her head still hurt but not as much. She tried to recall her conversation with the people who'd saved her, but this was fuzzy. They were old. That much she knew. So she needn't worry someone would come into the room and try to kiss her. Not that that was likely anyway. Who'd want to kiss someone with a bad headache?

The blackout curtains were drawn and Heike could barely see her foot. Her bare foot. The old people had taken off her shoes and socks and put her under an eiderdown. This was the best eiderdown she'd ever been under, puffy and white and light as air. Maybe the old people were elves. They looked a bit like elves, now that she thought about it. They were both tiny and had very blue eyes, twinkly and blue. Like elves. Elves of course weren't real, unless you were six. But there were people who looked like them. She'd just met two.

What time was it, Heike wondered. Probably still afternoon. A siren was going off though, so it must be later. Maybe seven. Time to go to the shelter. But where was the shelter? The house was only two stories high, she now remembered, and could a two-story house have a shelter big enough to house hundreds of people? It wouldn't need to though. Two story houses contained at most four people, maybe six if there were grandparents. Eight at most, with servants. Julia's apartment, much larger than this house, held three. And two servants. And an SS in the hallway. Heike wondered whether she should count the SS and decided she should. He had to sleep too. He probably came in at night and slept in one of the servants' rooms. So four, and two servants. But the apartment was twice as big.

She and Julia had explored it once, when the servants had a day off. The servants, she said, had been with them for years. Both were mutes. They could hear but they couldn't talk. Her father had saved them from going away and they felt grateful and were insanely loyal. That was Julia's phrase. Julia had told her something important, but Heike couldn't remember what. Something to do with…She couldn't remember. Her head hurt when she moved. Still, she had to get up soon. If it was time for the bombing, Mutti would be beside herself. And she'd take it out on Heike, even if she was relieved to see her. The sooner she got home the better.

Heike sat up and fell right back down again, with the world spinning. She thought she was going to throw up but drew her knees to her chest and breathed deeply, the way Hans had taught her. He said if you felt you were going to throw up, lie on your back with your knees up and nine times out of ten you wouldn't.

What about the tenth time, Heike had asked.

What? said Hans.

The tenth time you have knees up. What about that?

What about it, Hans said.

How come you throw up then?

You're a moron, said Hans.

No I'm not, Heike said, amazed and gratified once more at how easy it was to drive Hans crazy. You said nine times out of ten you wouldn't throw up. That means you would the tenth time. I just want to know is what's different the tenth time.

I was wrong, Hans said, red in the face with rage. You're not a moron. You're a Jew. You were switched at birth with an Aryan girl. Only Jews ask questions like that.

No. You said...

If you say that once more, I'll throw you out the window, Jew, said Hans.

I'm not a Jew, Heike complained. And you know it. You're just calling me that because you can't answer my question.

No. You're a Jew. You even look like one. Werner Kopflanger noticed it and I said he was seeing things but I now I see he was right.

Mutti, Heike screamed. Mutti, Hans called me a Jew.

What? came the shout from the kitchen.

He called me...

At this Hans had put his hand over her mouth, he was then twelve...she was eight... and used his weight to shuttle her towards an open window.

For some reason, at this moment, as the nausea was subsiding, Heike had the conviction that Hans was dead. It wasn't a silly feeling or anything like that. She didn't want him dead. She just knew he was and burst out crying. The crying re-ignited her nausea and she forced herself to stop. Between crying and throwing up and not crying and not throwing up, there was no contest. She didn't want to throw up. But the sense that Hans was dead impacted Heike's entire body, as if she had run into a wall.

The sirens had stopped and Heike waited for the bombers to arrive. This usually took no more than ten minutes. Fifteen at most. Sometimes, even twenty. She had ten minutes of guaranteed life, then she'd have to see. If the bombs fell too close, it might be necessary to crawl to the shelter. Assuming there was a shelter. She could call for help of course. Which reminded her, how come no one had come to help, since the sirens had already sounded. Maybe the elves had left the house. Maybe they'd even forgotten she was there, left, and by the time they remembered, it would be too late.

Heike felt panic rise in her stomach, taking the place of the nausea. But they couldn't have left, because, as she'd already remarked, they didn't have anywhere to go. Something else was going on. She should count to six hundred and then see what happened. Rather, she could count to four hundred eighty, since two minutes had passed since the sirens sounded, meaning 120 seconds had passed and 120 from 600 was 480. That's how Mutti had put her to sleep when Heiki was little. Mutti would come in the bedroom, sit by the bed and they'd add up the number of months Heike had been alive. Five times twelve is 60. But no self-respecting child could fall asleep by sixty so they would count weeks instead. If there were fifty two weeks in a year, and Heiki was five years old, that meant she had been alive for two hundred sixty weeks. That was better. Often, Heike was asleep by the time Mutti finished multiplying the numbers.

* * *

At nine hundred, Heike stopped counting. The bombers should have come. They hadn't. Something was trying to get her to remember it. If she could only get up, she could walk to the grandfather clock and check the time. It was too dark to see it from here and she still felt weak. Then she remembered. One of the elves, the male elf, said there would be a curfew. That's what the siren was. They always announced curfews, and everything else that was important, with sirens. That's how you knew it was important. A curfew meant you couldn't go out after it began, but it also meant you had time before the bombers came because they never came right after curfew. They came later, sometimes hours later. There had even been curfews when they hadn't come at all.

Heike again tried to sit up and this time succeeded. She felt a little nauseous but stifled it almost immediately, even without raising her legs. There was something else she wasn't thinking that she should have been. Hans. That's right. Once again, Heike burst into sobs, but this time, without feeling as if she was going to throw up. Hans had been a pig, but he was her brother, the only one she would ever have. She'd loved him in a way, especially when they were both little and he was so much stronger and smarter than she was. And he was nice at times, like when she was scared in the market and he took her hand, or when she didn't know how to get home and was standing in the street outside school and he came and got her and led her back. It was hard to believe he'd ever done these things and yet he had. And maybe he couldn't help it that he became a pig. Maybe that's what happened to all boys when they went through puberty...eecchhh, such an ugly word...Maybe they all became pigs.

Anyway, her path was clear. Hans's death had clarified it. She had to get back to Mutti, no matter what. She had to walk home and be there for her in case Mutti started to go crazy at the thought of Hans's death. Heike was confident her presence would calm Mutti and give her the strength to bear what had happened to Hans. Besides, he wasn't really Hans anymore. Any time anyone did something he didn't like, he called them a Jew. Jews were all he could think about. This person was probably a Jew and that one was certainly a Jew and if they took off his pants they'd find out. And he'd take off their pants one of these days and prove it. And so on. He had been Hans once upon a time, but then he wasn't.

Heike slid her legs over the edge of the bed and sat there, half on, half off. It was weird to feel this weak. She felt like she didn't have any muscles, just mass, mass without muscles. She had legs and a torso, and even the beginning of breasts. But no strength. It was weird. The room was spinning again, going round and round, from the painting of children ice skating she could now make out over the dresser, to the hard backed chair the woman elf had sat on, to the wash stand, to the painting again. She should lie back down. But this would make it completely impossible to ever get up and leave. If she lay down now, with the knowledge Hans was dead, she wouldn't be able to lift her body off the eiderdown, never mind off the feather mattress and completely off the bed. It was now or never.

That's right. Julia had been telling her about sex. Julia had just had sex. Today was the most complicated day of her, Heike's, life. First there was news that Hans was coming back, then Julia's sex, then Hans...no, first her concussion...then Hans's death. That was the right order. She should let her legs slip down until her feet touched the floor but still keep enough of her body on the mattress to allow her to lie back immediately in case she needed to. This should be easy enough. Just inch forward...Heike liked that expression. Inch forward. It appeared she was crying again...Inch forward a little more and...

Bang. She was falling. Or had fallen. Heike couldn't tell which. She was collapsing in a heap on the floor. She'd made a noise. Maybe her head had hit the floorboards and that's what made the sound. Anyway, the room wasn't spinning anymore. It was turning white, then gray, then totally black.

.4.

It was Trudi's job, prior to any expected heavy bombing, to alert the residents of the building and remind them to bring extra supplies to the bomb shelter. This was particularly inconvenient today, since Heike had not yet come home, the roast was bubbling on the burner, and Trudi had just had sex and very likely needed a shower. But there was no time to take a shower and still complete her other tasks. She washed as quickly and efficiently as possible, left a note for Heike on the front door, and walked up the wide, marble staircase, in the dark, to the 6th and top floor. She knocked first on the door of Herr Faber, whom very few people in the building had seen since his interrogation by the SS, and identified herself. A stirring behind the closed door told her Herr Faber was home and Trudi reminded him to bring an extra blanket tonight, and enough food for twenty four hours, in case they had to remain in the shelter past the normal time. There was no answer, as Trudi knew there wouldn't be, since, since the interrogation, Herr Faber hadn't been known to speak. Nonetheless, Trudi dutifully crossed him off her list.

After taking a deep breath, Trudi reversed direction and knocked on Frau Brest's door. For as long as anyone could remember, Frau Brest had inhabited this apartment. There were rumors she had been Herr Faber's mistress and it was this that prompted her to turn him in to the SS. Whatever her motivation, she and Herr Faber continued to live side by side in their garret apartments, separated by eleven feet of marble floor.

This floor, black tiles alternating with white, was barely visible in the faint glow of Trudi's flashlight as she waited for Frau Brest to answer the knock. Experience had taught her that Frau Brest would not ask who it was. Nor would you hear Frau Brest's footsteps as she approached the door. The door would open suddenly, as if by itself, and Frau Brest would be standing in it, large and implacable, waiting for you to make the first move.

Despite knowing this, it was always a shock to Trudi when it happened. The sight of Frau Brest, with her small eyes, large face, full jaw, and plastered down hair made Trudi momentarily tongue tied and she had to take a second breath before informing Frau Brest, who already knew it quite well, why she had come. Behind the woman, her apartment stretched into darkness. Trudi could make out a large object in the hallway, like a club or wooden sword, and could also isolate the form of two or more coats hanging from hangers. From Trudi's angle, it looked as if there were people in them.

After she finished her speech, Frau Brest said, Yes, you have discharged your duty like a good German citizen. I will bring what is necessary.

Trudi thanked her and was about to leave when Frau Brest asked if she had already spoken to the man in 3F, meaning Rolph.

Trudi said No, she hadn't, but as he was their air raid warden, she was certain he was aware of the new regulations.

Frau Brest said nothing, but held Trudi with her steely gaze.

Is there something else? Trudi asked, breaking the spell.

There is something strange, I think, about that one, Frau Brest said. He looks like an Aryan but I think there is something strange about him. You should be careful.

Trudi was about to ask why she in particular should be careful but prevented herself in time and thanked Frau Brest and started down the stairs to the fifth floor.

It was only when Trudi arrived at that floor that she realized her knees were shaking. She had to hold on to the banister for a moment before she could trust herself to walk. Frau Brest knew. She must have known. She certainly knew Trudi and Rolph were lovers. She had told her as much.

Realizing this was the worst possible time to lose self-control, Trudi roused herself and knocked on Frau Gleich's door. Who is it? Frau Gleich asked after a moment. Trudi told her and delivered the message to the closed entrance. Trudi could hear children asking Frau Gleich who is it, and Frau Gleich telling them to be quiet. Frau Gleich, Trudi knew, was conducting a romance with Klaus, the building Superintendent. A smell of cooking meat often drifted out from under Frau Gleich's door, despite the dish towels she too continually packed under the door frame. Frau Gleich was a short, heavyset woman with beetling eyebrows and a permanent squint. What the superintendent saw in her was a source of constant speculation for the more gossip-minded of the building residents. Some imagined she was blackmailing Klaus. Others attributed his attraction to displaced mother anxieties. No one could explain how they could have sex while Frau Gleich was at the same time tending four small, often screaming, children.

Trudi next knocked on the Febelweichers door. Herr and Frau Febelweicher were both hard of hearing so Trudi knocked forcefully and continued to knock until Herr Febelweicher answered. He was holding a pistol, which caused Trudi to skip quickly to one side of the doorway before explaining why she was there. A poster of the Fuhrer was tacked over a secretary just inside the Febelweicher entrance.

Herr Febelweicher said Yes, he would be certain to bring reading material to the shelter, perhaps the Fuhrer's latest speech, and Trudi, after several more attempts, gave up trying to explain the situation to him and crossed him off her list. It must be a curse to be hard of hearing, she told herself, taking the next flight of stairs. Although it would certainly come in handy at times. For example, last night, it would have come in handy. It would have allowed her to pretend she hadn't understood what Rolph was saying. This afternoon, however, when she and Rolph were making small but intense, if not condensed and violent, noises during sex, deafness would have lessened her pleasure considerably. Trudi colored, and felt a stirring in her groin. Again? So soon? she said to herself as she reached the fourth floor landing.

The fourth floor contained four apartments and Trudi moved through them with dispatch. The Shickerdiensts, another elderly couple, thanked her profusely for warning them as Frau Shickerdienst was ill and needed to take medication at four hour intervals or be prone to seizures. This wasn't guaranteed, Herr Shickerdeinst said, as Trudi tried to depart as gracefully as possible, but it happened often enough that they never went anywhere without first making certain they'd brought her medicine. Once they had gone to Murnau on vacation and when they arrived at their hotel, Frau Schickerdeinst discovered she had left her medicine at home.

Trudi shook her head, said How terrible, and added that he must tell her the entire story another time, possibly tonight, in the shelter. Herr Schickerdeinst was still standing in his doorway as Trudi roused Frau Meldt who said, Yes, she was aware there would be heavy bombing tonight and she had prepared blankets and food for herself and her son, Angus, now Walther, the two of them having changed his name when Angus/Walther's English father left them high and dry immediately after the invasion of Czechoslovakia. Across the way, Fraulein Hessenkirche and her sister said they couldn't come to the door right now so could Trudi either please tell them what to do or slide a flyer under their door. This was one of the few apartments Trudi had been in. The Hessenkirches collected African art and their apartment was filled with African masks which frightened and disturbed Trudi, although she was always careful to hide this. The sisters were tall, very thin, and always dressed in gray knee length smocks with white stockings. Both wore their gray hair in braids.

Next was the Smoltz apartment. Frau Smoltz too had heard they could expect a heavy bombing and told Trudi not to worry, she had read the tarot and it told her they would all live through the night. In fact, she could say with authority that both she and Trudi would survive the entire war.

Next was Floor 3. Trudi didn't bother to knock on Rolph's door. He was out, and, besides... Frau Benzinger and her two young daughters expressed alarm when Trudi explained that they might need additional supplies. The siren indicating the onset of Curfew sounded in the middle of Trudi's explanation and the two girls, blond, blue eyed, with startled expressions and very light, almost white eyebrows, clutched their mother around her thighs and stared at Trudi as though she was responsible for the siren. Their dark-haired mother put an arm around each slight pair of shoulders and pulled the girls to her, cooing

Frau Engstahl occupied the apartment directly across from Rolph's. Trudi knocked and waited. She knew full well she was jealous of Frau Engstahl's relation to her daughter, although she wasn't certain what that was. Or why she should be jealous of it. Frau Engstahl was beautiful enough for women to be jealous of her without further reasons. She had an effortless, unselfconscious beauty, a beauty all the more disconcerting for her never seeming to flaunt it. She took what she received from men as a matter of course, without ever altering the frank, open way she spoke to everyone. It was she Rolph should have been involved with, Trudi thought, waiting for Frau Engstahl to open the door. She was beautiful, tragic, intelligent, not sexual perhaps, but her skin was perfect and she had lovely eyes.

That Rolph preferred Trudi, Trudi felt, was one more example of how, in the end, the sex drive is out of our hands. We think we choose our sexual partners, but a deeper power chooses for us. How else explain fat men with gorgeous women, or young men with much older ones.

Frau Engstahl opened the door, smiled and said, Oh Frau Meitner. You have come about the air raid, No?

Trudi said she had and would Frau Engstahl remember to bring extra food and blankets...

Frau Engstahl pointed to a small wrapped packet, sitting by the door. There is my food, she said. I always bring a blanket. It's so damp down there, don't you think?

Trudi agreed it was damp and made to go.

Frau Engstahl stopped her.

Should we write out names on our arms? Frau Meitner?

Yes, said Trudi. And your next of kin, please. If you don't have next of kin, a dear friend will do.

Suppose we have neither, Frau Engstahl said with a small smile. Should we write the Fuhrer?

Trudi was about to respond when she realized it was a joke and she too smiled.

He will be too busy, I think. Someone nearer by, maybe.

Frau Engstahl laughed. Yes. Closer. And how is your daughter? I haven't seen her for weeks.

She's fine, Trudi said. She's been seeing a lot of her friend, Julia.

Ah, Frau Engstahl said. It's such a shame girls these days lead such pressured lives.

Yes, it is, Trudi said, wondering what she meant.

Well. Thank you for alerting me to the air raid, Frau Engstahl said, stepping back from the door.

Trudi turned away, then turned back. Frau Smoltz, she blurted out, in 4F?, read the Tarot and said it said we will all be all right tonight, Trudi trailed off, feeling very stupid.

That's good to know, Frau Engstahl replied, and once again both women smiled.

You don't believe in Tarot? Trudi asked.

This is another case where it makes no difference what I believe. Or what Tarot says. If we live, Frau Smoltz will say the

Tarot told us we would, and if we die, none of us will be around to reproach it.

Trudi laughed, liking Frau Engstahl in spite of herself.

I hope we live. Heike was supposed to be home by four but she isn't back yet. Or wasn't when I left. I didn't hear the downstairs door open.

Frau Engstahl nodded, waiting for Trudi to go on.

She went to Julia's, and she's usually back earlier than this.

There are a million reasons she might not have come back, Frau Meitner, Frau Engstahl said.

I know. I tell myself that, but I can't help worrying. Thinking the worst, even.

No, Frau Engstahl agreed. Do you want to come in and talk for a moment?

I can't, Trudi said. I have to finish.

Well, if you do, I'm here. And there's always the shelter, Frau Engstahl said, calm and graceful as always.

Trudi nodded.

Teenage girls lose track of time, Frau Engstahl continued as Trudi once more turned to go. Their brains don't seem to have the capacity to remember where they are. I teach them, and even when they are physically present, they're somewhere else. Julia may have talked Heike into going somewhere and they simply forgot about the curfew.

Yes. Thank you. That is probably what happened, Trudi said.

She'll come back, Frau Engstahl said. But visit me if you have time. I'll make us tea.

I will, Trudi said.

* * *

Trudi completed the remaining floors as quickly as possible. Her apartment was empty when she returned, although Herr Gruber had followed her up the stairs, asking one transparently silly question after another until Trudi realized why and invited him in to share the roast. Hungry as she now was, the roast barely touched her consciousness. Neither of her children had come home when both were expected.

The roast, when Trudi examined it, was done. The meat fell

off the bone at the slightest touch and all the cooking liquid had been absorbed. As she turned to find a spatula, Trudi's elbow collided with Herr Gruber, who had crept up behind and was peering over her shoulder into the pot. He held his eye socket and Trudi apologize profusely for having elbowed it, but secretly, she was pleased she had. The last thing in the world she wanted in her present mood was to share her worries, never mind her meal, with Herr Gruber. She wanted to be alone. She wanted to be out on the street, looking for Heike. Hans could take care of himself. But there was a curfew. And a roast. And she couldn't.

.5.

Instead, Trudi invited Frau Engstahl and the Hessenkirches to join her and Herr Gruber. She set the table with her best silver, the silver they'd received from Alfred's family on their wedding day, and her best China. Chipped though they were, the Meissen plates retained the elegance that had made Trudi buy them, against Alfred's wishes, while she was still a young wife. Flowers wound around the plates' edge, intertwined with one another in a never-ending sequence of blues and pinks and yellows and greens, all muted, all fading into one another like spring.

Trudi arranged the table so that Frau Engstahl sat to her right, and the elder Frau Hessenkirche, Greta, to her left. Herr Gruber sat across the table, the white napkin tucked in the v of his plaid shirt. Nula Hessenkriche sat between her sister and Herr Gruber.

Herr Gruber offered to carve but Trudi said she would carve and proceeded to do so. The meat was soft and pliant and fell away in chunks rather than smooth slices. The smells it released were overpoweringly delicious and even the Hessenkirche sisters, normally staid and immovably self-contained, reacted to them. This was food. What they were meant to eat, what human beings were meant to eat.

Trudi brought the tray with the meat and two potatoes to the table and proceeded to serve each of her guests roast pork. She served Nula first, then Greta, then Frau Engstahl, then Herr Gruber, and last, herself. After this, she cut the potatoes into thirds and put a third on each plate. She covered the potato and meat with the little gravy she'd managed to salvage from the bottom of the pot, and sat.

All this took place in silence, as though it were happening at Church. Like the Hessenkirche sisters, Frau Engstahl couldn't completely hide how moved she was to be served meat. Only Trudi's attention was elsewhere. But she was the hostess. So she said to everyone: Eat.

Herr Gruber cut into his roast and raised a forkful to his mouth. Bless This Meal, he said, a look of pure bliss washing over his face. The others ate with the concentration of people who hadn't had a good meal in a long time…

In a few seconds, Herr Gruber had cleared his plate of food. He then stared at it with a good natured if somewhat baffled expression, slid his chair back, and clasped his hands over his stomach.

Aaahhh, he said.

Trudi glanced at his plate, thought briefly of putting some of her own meat on it, rejected the idea, and bolted down the rest of her braised roast. The Hessenkirche sisters were still eating, forcing themselves to take as small bites as possible. Frau Engstahl was almost finished. She too had eaten quickly, though not as quickly as Trudi and Herr Gruber. Her potato lay on her plate, surrounded by a thin layer of juice from her slice of meat. Herr Gruber couldn't keep his eyes off it and, to prevent him from arousing sufficient sympathy for Frau Engstahl to offer him some, Trudi asked him where he'd been born.

Gottingen, said Herr Gruber. I am a Gottingen child. Such a lovely city. You've been there, Frau Meitner?

What did you parents do, Herr Gruber? Trudi asked, shaking her head.

My father was a surveyor and my beloved mother, her name too was Trudi, was a mother and housewife. She had seven children. I was the seventh and so, the youngest. I was spoiled. I was six before I saw my first Jew.

Here, Herr Gruber sighed. His blue eyes seemed to film over and, for a moment, Trudi wondered what it would be like to pick up the carving knife and stick it in the soft spot just under his sternum.

Yes. Herr Gruber continued, as the Hessenkirche sisters finished their meal and used the last of their potato to soak up the gravy, Gottingen was a small city, with very few Jews. Still, we used to joke, what is the difference between a Jew and a...

What did your father survey? interposed Frau Engstahl, smiling at Herr Gruber, who returned her smile with simple but all-encompassing egotism.

You will think I'm bragging, Fraulein, but Papa was chief surveyor in charge of the Schwarzwald Essen Highway, Herr Gruber said...

Frau, Frau Engstahl corrected him, with a warm smile. Not Fraulein.

Yes, and therefore, in his own small way, Papa made it

possible for our troops to move east with dispatch.

That must have been gratifying for him, Frau Engstahl continued, as the sound of a tank convoy rose from the street below. This, Trudi noted, was the third of the past hour, the third tank convoy to have passed their building.

Unfortunately, Papa died before he could see the fruit of his work, Herr Gruber said, so it was left to my six siblings and myself to celebrate it.

This was delicious, Nula Hessenkirche told Trudi, and blushed. This meal has made me believe in life again.

Life, Herr Gruber said. You see? Here I am, talking about death, when all around us there is Life.

How did he die? Herr Gruber, asked Frau Engstahl.

He was run over, Herr Gruber replied. A giant truck backed up, ran him over and...Poof. Papa was so absorbed in reviewing new construction plans with his foreman that he didn't see it coming.

Was the foreman also killed? asked the elder Hessenkirche sister.

I don't remember, said Herr Gruber, knitting his brow. This is odd, but I can no longer even remember his name...the foreman's name. For many years, it was printed on my memory.

It is sad to lose a parent while you are still a child, Frau Engstahl said into the silence that followed.

Yes, Herr Gruber agreed. For many months, I shut myself up and would only listen to lieder. Which is how I learned to sing lieder.

Will you sing some for us? asked the two Hessenkirche as one.

There was a soft knock on the door which no one appeared to notice.

Lieder must not be performed within a half hour of eating and drinking, Herr Gruber said. I learned this from my teacher, Frau Marx.

Marx, repeated Nula Hessenkirche. Jewish?

I was too small to know at the time, Herr Gruber said.

No one would think of blaming you, said Nula Hessenkirche.

You must remember, Herr Gruber said, there was a time in the recent past when Jews were a common sight in our cities. Even an old man like myself, with poor eyesight, could spot them.

How? asked Frau Engstahl.

They wore a star, Trudi said.

Before the star, my dear Frau Meitner, said Herr Gruber. I am not that young. They gave off an aura which I was able to detect. I thought if little Herman Gruber could do this, anyone could. I remember one day walking with Mutti in Kaiser Platz when I was six years of age and I said , Look Mutti, across the Platz. Jews.

How do you know they're Jews, Mutti said. I can barely see them.

They have halos, I said.

Herr Gruber laughed merrily.,

What did your mother say? Trudi asked.

This is why I laughed, Frau Meitner. She cuffed me. She said, Jews don't have halos.

Why not, Mutti? I asked through tears.

Because they killed our Lord, she said. She was very angry with me. You should have seen her.

But, Herr Gruber, I thought you said there were no Jews in Gottingen, said Frau Engstahl, with perfect neutrality. Or almost no Jews.

Bravo!, Herr Gruber said. You remembered. This is what made my talent so...so noteworthy, Fraulein. There weren't. But I was able to distinguish what few Jews there were even though they did their best to look like Aryans. It was a gift.

Do you still have it, Herr Gruber? the elder Hessenkirche asked.

Herr Gruber inclined his head. Since my wife died, I don't like to talk about it, he said, refolding his hands over his stomach.

That must mean he does!, the younger Hessenkirche blurted out.

Herr Gruber sighed, but didn't reply and another silence came over the table.

And where were you born, Frauleinen? Frau Engstahl turned to the two women as very light, almost inaudible knocking continued to play at the door. Herr Gruber thought he might have heard something but was loathe to chance admitting another guest to their party for fear it would be a male who would upstage him. Since his wife's death, no one but Heike had paid serious attention to him. So tonight was a rare treat, on several counts.

We were born in Heidelburg, said the elder Hessenkirche. We moved here when we twelve.

Yes, and I was ten, the younger chimed in.

What a lovely age, Herr Gruber said. German girls are at their best at twelve. Before they become German women, the most beautiful in Europe.

All four women smiled at Herr Gruber, who raised a hand as if waving off their thanks.

Our parents were clerks at the University, the eldest sister continued. Our father in the Department of Philosophy and our mother in the Medical Department.

Our mother also baked pastries, the younger Hessenkirche said, and sold them at weekend markets. They became famous...

Nula, her older sister said, reprovingly.

She made the best kirchertorte, Nula continued, ignoring her sister's warning. Hessenkirche Kirchertorte.

Nula giggled. We used to accompany Mutti to market to help her sell. If we arrived at ten, the kirchentorte were completely gone by noon. People would drive in from surrounding villages to buy Mutti's kirchentorte. At Christmas, she decorated each cake with a little sugar star...

A five-pointed star, I hope, Herr Gruber said.

And the little children would fight with each other for the star. Mutti put vanilla in the sugar, that was her secret. And a tiny bit of brandy in the dough. She said it made the dough lively because dough, in itself, is fat and slow.

Frau Engstahl, to whom the younger Hessenkirche had addressed herself, nodded and asked if their mother baked anything else.

Apple dumplings, the elder Hessenkirche murmured.

It must have been hard for you to move from a beautiful town like Heidelburg to a huge city like ours, Frau Engstahl observed.

We had to, Nula Hessenkirche blurted out. Father lost his job...

Nula!, Greta said.

Still, Frau Engstahl said gently, for whatever reason...

It was very difficult, the elder sister admitted. We had many friends in Heidelburg and we were known there. When we came to our new home, no one knew us and school, the first year of school, was very difficult.

We had barely any money, her sister put in.

This was nothing. It was the social aspect...

We were always hungry. Then Papa found a job with the Ministry.

What a relief that must have been, Frau Engstahl said, her beautiful face expressing the relief the sisters must have felt. Trudi stared at Frau Engstahl, once more seeing what had entranced Heike. Trudi herself had fallen under her spell and was no longer worried that Heike hadn't returned home. As Frau Engstahl said, she had probably lost track of time and stayed at Julia's until it was too late to leave.

Yes. He lost his job because of his politics, Nula continued.

I forbid you, Greta began...

You see, Papa joined the Socialist Party right after the Putsch. He understood from the very beginning what was happening to our country...

That is enough Nula!, Gerta almost shouted.

Nula looked like she'd been slapped. Trudi was about to speak when Frau Engstahl said this has been an extremely difficult time for all of them. No one knew where their next meal would come from and everyone turned to whoever they felt would do best for Germany.

I myself was confused, Herr Gruber said, as if this settled the matter. First I joined the Socialist Nationalist Party, then the Nationalists, then the Socialists. It was not until '33 that I joined the National Socialists. Even then, I wasn't completely certain I had made the right choice. My beloved wife would say, Herman, people like you are not political. We should let sleeping dogs lie. But, Liebschen, I would say to her, I remember this as if it was yesterday, I would say, Liebschen, how can we let sleeping dogs lie when Jews charge a billion marks for a loaf of bread? Someone must stop them, even if it means we eat less well.

Once again Trudi suppressed an impulse to find a heavy pan and brain Herr Gruber with it. It wasn't true that the Jews charged a billion marks for bread. Or rather, it was true, but at that time, everyone charged a billion marks. Certainly the Jews created certain social problems, but this was because of their clannishness, or the outlandishness of the way some of them dressed, or their disproportionate representation at Universities.

Not because they overcharged for food. Besides, while there were Jewish butchers and grocers, many more were Aryan. And many of these charged more than their Jewish counterparts.

The knocking had stopped and Herr Gruber, taking the silence which greeted his last comment for assent, leaned back and allowed himself a contented sigh. Yes. This might be his last night on earth. Although he didn't think so. But if it was, he had acquitted himself well. He had had a lovely meal, with four lovely women. He had talked about his life with adults for the first time since his wife died. He had even listened to the women describe their lives, pure, good German lives, and now it was time to go to the shelter and claim the spot he always claimed during heavy bombings. Yet, as he pushed back his chair, Herr Gruber suddenly choked up. It must, he thought, have something to do with his beloved wife. If only she was still alive to see him, to feel proud of the way he had comported himself. If only she were still here, he could refrain from pleasuring himself for a few days in the hopes she would consent to be intimate. Even well into her seventies, this had happened. She would insist they turn out all the lights, the poor, modest dear, but once the lights were extinguished, she would become her old self, moaning and screaming with pleasure as he hunted down all her secret places…

Yes, Herr Gruber sighed, deliberately bringing himself up short as he couldn't very well rise from the table with an erection, yes, as much as he would have liked his wife back, she was dead. Death, the mysterious claimant of everyone, Jew and gentile alike, had taken her and wouldn't give her back. Herr Gruber coughed back a sob and his erection disappeared.

Meine Frauleinen, Frau Meitner, he began, rising from the table as someone knocked, loudly now, on the Meitner door.

Herr Gruber sat back down. Trudi got up and opened the door without asking who it was and Rolph entered, looking tired.

Are you all right? Trudi asked.

Yes, fine, Rolph said, blankly taking in the scene before him.

I didn't save you any roast, Trudi wailed.

I ate, said Rolph. Hello Herr Gruber.

I was just leaving, meine Herr, Herr Gruber said, rising for the second time and tipping the trilby hat for which he was famous.

Rolph. Did you know Herr Gruber can tell if someone is

a Jew, Trudi said out loud to her own astonishment and the astonishment of the others.

Really, said Rolph.

Yes. He can see their aura.

Remarkable, Rolph added, staring at Trudi.

So, before we say goodbye, Herr Gruber, can you tell us if any of us here has any Jewish blood.

Herr Gruber smiled at Rolph, as an older man smiles at a younger one when he wants to acknowledge the strangeness of the opposite sex.

Well, he said, from the time I was little, as I told the fraulien, I have been able to detect a Jew simply by looking at him. Once this became known, the Gestapo arranged a test for me. They brought me to their headquarters and had me examine twenty people, all of whom looked exactly alike. Well, I say exactly but of course you cannot take this literally, since, unless you are an identical twin, nature has arranged that each one of us has small distinguishing features which make us what we are.

Here Herr Gruber paused and waited a moment before continuing. Whenever I tell this story, people would say to me, Weren't you afraid, Herr Gruber? What if you had failed? After all, the people you confronted looked just like one another. And I would say, No. I was never afraid because I believed in myself. The man who believes in himself as I did cannot fail.

So you identified the Jews, said Nula Hessenkirche breathlessly, one hand on her sternum.

Yes They were all Jews!, Herr Gruber exclaimed, triumphantly.

What? the Hessenkirche said as one.

The Gestapo presented me with twenty Jews who would seem to the average person to be Aryans, each and every one of them. I identified them at once as Jews. I turned to the Leiter in command and said, Herr Kommandant, you have shown me twenty Jews. He was about to contradict me when the officers standing behind us, several young, handsome SS, broke into applause.

Trudi stopped listening. She felt as if she might leave her body and forced herself to remain in the room only by gripping the edge of the table. When the moment passed, she let her gaze fall first on the Hessenkirche sisters, then on Frau Engstahl, then on Rolph, and finally, on Herr Gruber. She knew at once that the Hessenkirchen and Frau Engstahl would die that night. She tried to tell herself she was being hysterical, but no amount of reasoning could convince her she was wrong. She knew it, the way she knew the names of her children. There was no room for debate. It would have made no sense

Her heart began to beat faster as she examined herself for premonitions about Herr Gruber. Just as he could tell who was Jewish, she could now tell who would die. She found, however, she couldn't be certain about Herr Gruber. And when she summoned the courage to gaze at Rolph, she was certain he would live and breathed a sigh of relief.

This left Trudi herself, and, about herself, she couldn't say. She felt she might die, and she might not. But this was the case every night. You might die. You might live. If you lived, you might die the next night. She might have died the day her parents let her swim in the Aare and a current swept her away. Her brother had rescued her. She might have been run over by tanks if a man hadn't pulled her out of the street in time. She might have been killed by falling plaster if she'd sat one foot to her right in the shelter. You could always die. But these women, Trudi knew, would die tonight.

Trudi felt nothing about the Hessenkirchen. They were old, and had lived as much as they needed to. If they died this evening, they would miss nothing except what they had already missed. So their deaths didn't matter to Trudi, except in the way one always wants people to live.

Frau Engstahl was another story. Trudi glanced at her again to determine if her premonition was still present. It was, but it wasn't a premonition. It was a fact, although how could it be, since it predicted the future? And the future by definition was what one couldn't predict. Trudi asked herself what she should do? Should she tell Frau Engstahl? But if she told her, the news might influence her behavior in such a way that it would bring about what Trudi most feared. Frau Engstahl might do some-thing which ensured her death rather than evaded it. Her death would then rest at Trudi's doorstep. Yet to not tell her seemed unthinkable. Because suppose a simple warning, not to sit there or there, would have saved her life? And Trudi wanted her to live.

Frau Engstahl noticed Trudi staring at her and smiled. Trudi tried to smile back. Herr Gruber was making his slow way around the table. He was talking, but Trudi heard nothing. She did notice a bit of gravy lodged at the corner of his mouth. If Herr Gruber had known, he would have licked it off and again commented on how delicious Trudi's roast was. Let it stay there, Trudi thought, getting up and walking around the table toward Frau Engstahl. Frau Engstahl had also gotten to her feet and was now shaking hands with Herr Gruber. Frau Engstahl's face wore the compassionate and accepting expression it always wore, as though her understanding of life was large enough even for a person such as this one. It was unthinkable that someone as rare and special as Frau Engstahl was about to die.

Then the Hessenkirchen shook hands with Herr Gruber and the three of them exchanged good byes, even though they would see one another again in a matter of moments. The air raid sirens hadn't sounded, but it was now six o'clock, and fully dark. It wouldn't be long.

Rolph was the last person to accept Herr Gruber's farewell. Rolph's face wore a grave and ironic cast, the latter buried deeply enough that only Trudi, and perhaps Frau Engstahl, saw it. He looked exceptionally handsome as he bent his head slightly to accept Herr Gruber' salutations. Trudi still couldn't tell if either of them would live through the night. She couldn't tell but she prayed with all her might that if one of them didn't, it would be Herr Gruber. This was awful. You couldn't pray for someone's death. But she prayed that if one of them had to die, it wouldn't be Rolph.

Herr Gruber had finished with Rolph and at last turned to Trudi. The moment their hands touched, she could once again hear his voice. This coming into and out of focus had ceased to surprise Trudi. The entire night had been surprising…astonishing even…although what, really, had happened?

…I will always remember this meal, Herr Gruber was saying to the assembled. Anyone who has lived as long as I have has eaten many roasts, hundreds, perhaps even thousands, but this, my dear Frauner Meitner, this is the one I will remember as long as I live: a precious German roast made by a precious German woman.

V: THE LOST TRIBE

.1.

A few moments ago, Trudi had been passionately in love with Rolph. Now, filing into the shelter with the building's other residents, these were her thoughts: Jews were a noise you imagined was coming from outside until you shut all the windows, put dishtowels under the doors and turned on the radio. Only then did you realize that the noise was coming from inside.

That was the Jew. At first, he felt like nothing so much as an external, an outlier, an alien. Then one day you awoke, pushed aside your eiderdown, swung your legs over the edge of the trundle bed, and realized in a blinding flash that he had taken possession of some vital part of yourself. You couldn't get him out if you tried. You could banish him, deport him, co-opt his business, steal his money, taboo all references to his religion, his place of work, his writings, his music, what have you...and yet even then you couldn't fully extirpate him. He would remain somewhere, deep inside you, waiting for the right moment to emerge.

The shelter was already largely full and Trudi's usual place, the place Heike habitually reserved for her, was occupied when she arrived. Herr Gruber gestured for Trudi to join him but she was reluctant to. He was seated next to Frau Brest and almost nothing could persuade Trudi to camp near that woman. Rolph was busy. Frau Engstahl too was busy. Frau Engstahl had taken on herself the task of visiting known hysterics and giving them a soothing homeopathic compound of her own composition in order to calm their nerves prior to the sounds of the first explosions. The Hessenkirchen sat against the far wall, knitting. However, they were doomed. One wouldn't want to be near them when their fate arrived.

A familiar, harmless face peered up at her and Trudi took the empty spot beside it without first registering that the face belonged to Herr Faber, the man Frau Brest had betrayed to the SS. Once she realized who it was, Trudi had to suppress an impulse to get up and find another seat. It would hurt the poor man's feelings. Better to stay and endure his presence for the short time they would be together. Or the long time. Or the eternity even. There was nothing inherently objectionable after all about Herr Faber. It was simply that you didn't want to be near him.

I apologize, Herr Faber interrupted Trudi's thoughts in a soft, recessed, half swallowed voice. It was I who knocked on your door.

I'm sorry, Trudi replied distractedly. When was this? Good evening to you, Herr Faber.

Good evening, Frau Meitner. I wasn't certain I should knock, but as you were so kind as to knock on my own door with information about tonight's air raid,...

Rolph passed by. He walked in the determined way he always walked when he was on duty. Determined, and even officious. No, not officious. Official. More official than officious. Trudi couldn't have had sex with someone who was officious.

When no one answered, I thought perhaps everyone inside had died, Herr Faber continued. But I no longer have the physical strength to knock loudly. Frau Nuland heard me. You know Frau Nuland? She lives across the hall from you.

Of course, Trudi said, trying to concentrate on what Faber was saying.

She's the one with the parrot. The occupant on the other side of her, is Frau Schmitz. Frau Schmitz never comes out of her apartment. Not since her husband died. He drove a tank. He was run over by our own command car, you must have heard, That was how he died. He was relieving himself and they didn't see him. A tragedy, Herr Faber said, making an odd sucking noise with his mouth.

Trudi bit her lower lip. She began to understand why Frau Brest might have denounced him. Every fiber of his being, it seemed to Trudi, asked you to.

...Schmitz screamed all night, Herr Faber was saying. I am surprised you didn't hear it. I am directly above her, however, and perhaps this is the reason I heard it but you and most other residents of our building were unable to hear it. Sound travels upward, and Frau Schmitz and I share a common air shaft. Sometimes I hear things I think I shouldn't.

No doubt, Trudi thought. All of us hear things we shouldn't. This is what makes life interesting.

As if to confirm this observation, Trudi looked around the packed shelter. People had settled in and were decorating their cramped space with blankets, books, food, candles, tending to children, to animals, to themselves. How many of them had denounced a neighbor to the SS? How many had hid a neighbor? How many had committed adultery, as she had, or stolen, or murdered, unlikely as that was. How many had done something they would tell no-one, but might one day reveal in a dream, waking the person next to them and startling that person, a person who, until that moment, thought they knew everything there was to know about them.

…may have heard that I was interrogated by the State Security Police, Faber's voice once more overrode Trudi's thoughts. They were polite and careful with me, Herr Faber continued, but the experience unsettled me so deeply that I would stay at home all day while most other residents would go out. This is how I happened to be home when Frau Schmitz received news her husband had been run over. My first thought was: someone is being murdered.

It's all right, Herr Faber, Trudi said. No one expected you to rush downstairs and prevent a murder. After all, you were still uncertain of what you heard.

Ah, Herr Faber said hopefully, looking up. You understand.

Yes, Trudi replied, pulling out her blanket and wrapping it around her legs, but if you don't mind, perhaps you could tell me the rest of the story later. Once the bombing is over. I like to prepare myself before the planes come.

No-one need worry, Frau Meitner, said Herr Faber. I know that I talk too much. I have been silent so long that when I have a chance to speak with another human being, I cannot stop myself. It is a weakness I am all too conscious of. This is why people avoid me. They realize they will be a captive audience. I too realize this. I tell myself, be quiet now. You are boring these poor people. Look at them yawn and turn their heads. And yet much of the time, I am incapable of stopping myself. It is though I am possessed.

Trudi smiled at him and turned her gaze toward the door in the hope Heike might have come in. They were getting ready to close the doors—huge steel affairs that had been installed three months into the bombing. There was a dispute among residents as to whether the doors would keep ordnance out or, if there was a direct hit on the building, seal those in the shelter in. There was no way to resolve the dispute short of an actual test case, which neither side wanted.

At first, Herr Faber said, unable, as he had warned Trudi, to stop himself from talking, I thought they had come for me because of a misconception. I told the gentlemen who drove me to headquarters that they could not possibly imagine I was anything but an Aryan, despite how I look.

Trudi nodded politely as the first bomb exploded, sounding as if someone had dropped a large book on a rug.

She shuddered.

You cannot always tell a book by its cover, I told them and while it's true I am small and have a somewhat large nose, my Aryan ancestry has been traced back five generations.

A string of bombs detonated, miles away. You could tell they were miles away. Their reports were muted, no louder and no softer than the initial report. Perhaps Rolph will come sit by me, Trudi thought, drawing the blanket up to her chest and tucking the bottom around her legs. The concrete was cold but more than giving her warmth, the blanket comforted her. Tucked in, she could believe her children were all right. There was no reason they shouldn't be. Because they had had nothing to do with it! Neither had she. It had been carried out without their knowledge or approval. They were, all three of them, to all intents and purposes, innocent.

Did you say something, Frau Meitner?

What? No. I just moved a bit.

Yes, said Herr Faber. I could tell they believed me but they were only messengers, young men dispatched to bring me in. What should I tell them?, I asked. You searched my apartment. You know I am hiding no-one.

More bombs fell. Closer now but still quite a ways off. Trudi leaned forward and clasped her arms around her knees. A deathly quiet had descended on the shelter. The adults were looking at the ceiling with intense concentration, as though, if they tried hard enough they could see through it.

More bombs, and the lights dimmed. There were a few

gasps. Trudi caught sight of Frau Engstahl. She was on her haunches, feeding something to a young girl. The girl's face was wet with tears. She too had had nothing to do with it. Why were they taking it out on her? Boom, she said aloud, and the people nearest her glanced over.

Trudi burped. The burp brought up a parody of the roast and she swallowed to calm her stomach. It's the children, she said aloud, as someone knelt beside her. Frau Engstahl? But it was Rolph.

Are you all right?, he asked.

Heike didn't come home, Trudi said.

Rolph nodded. He took her hand and held it. This was strange, given people were looking. Or could look if they wanted to.

I'm so worried about my children, Trudi said.

I know, Rolph said. Be patient. Heike is ok. A man came and said she was staying with them.

What?, said Trudi. What man? Where was this?

He lives in the Mews. I don't know any more. I have to go, Rolph said, releasing her hand and standing as bombs fell, much closer this time. The lights flickered off, causing everyone to gasp, then came back on, catching their startled faces.

Look for me at the All Clear, Rolph said. And was gone. Trudi rose to follow him, but a bomb fell nearby and she sat down. The mother instinct, she said aloud. Bombs were falling closer. Wouldn't it be ironic, Trudi thought, if they killed the last Jew in Berlin. She kept this thought to herself. No point in making trouble. Besides, if a bomb killed Rolph, it would probably kill me too. His secret would die with me.

Trudi laughed and hugged herself. Rolph had said Heike was alive. Bombs were falling steadily now. Some nights you knew the bombers were flying away from you. Towards someone else, but away from you. Tonight, everyone knew they were coming for them. For us. For the Hessenkirchen and Frau Engstahl and others.

Again, Trudi felt a tremendous urge to tell Frau Engstahl about her premonition. It was unfair of her not to, she decided, getting to her feet as the sound of bombs falling nearby produced small concussions that dislodged dust from the ceiling, causing it to fall in thin streams through the flickering lights. Flashlights had come on and were scraping the ceiling, searching for where pieces of concrete might have loosened. Be careful, people were telling one another.

The lights went out again, this time for good. A few battery-operated lanterns came on and Trudi used their light to pick her way through the mass of bodies sitting or lying on the floor.

Frau Engstahl, Trudi called, realizing she didn't know Frau Engstahl's first name. No one responded. She stepped on someone's leg but the person ignored her. Ignored her apology. Did she apologize? Had she said she was sorry?

A bomb exploded nearby, its concussion knocking Trudi off her feet. She fell on a fat woman, who pushed her off onto the heavyset woman to her left. This woman helped Trudi regain her balance.

Stay here, the heavyset said. Sit. It's dangerous to walk.

Trudi obeyed, gradually realizing she'd been on the verge of hysteria. She thanked the second woman and leaned against a column, listening with the others for the next explosion. It came later than she and they expected, late enough that many residents thought the bombers had passed. First there was a sudden drop in air pressure, followed immediately by an equally sudden rise in pressure accompanied by noise that obliterated everyone's hearing. The building shook, stabilized, then began to shed giant sections of its concrete ceiling.

Screams punctuated the collapse, becoming a crescendo of screams as Trudi's hearing gradually returned.

Trudi stood up, brushed herself off, then reached down to help the heavyset woman, who was dead, crushed by a wedge of falling concrete. Backing away from the dead woman, Trudi turned and saw a wall of flame where the steel doors had been. The sight confused and paralyzed her and she stood rooted to the spot until and hand grabbed her arm and someone said, Follow me.

Trudi complied, suddenly unable to see more than a foot in front of her.

Don't rub your eyes, the voice commanded. Again, Trudi obeyed, aware that a wind was now blowing in her face. Which was impossible because how could wind blow in a sealed space?

I'm going to carry you. Put your arms around my neck. Trudi felt herself lifted off her feet. Rolph?, she said. Hold on, he said. We're almost there.

* * *

Outside, smoke billowed from parts of the building that had remained standing after the direct hit. The rest of structure lay in an insane jumble of wood, steel, and concrete. As her sight returned, Trudi could make out people picking over the rubble, some deliberate, some frantically calling out names and pulling helplessly at whatever they could get their hands on. Sirens sounded in every direction.

Stay here, Rolph said. I'll come back for you as soon I can.

No, said Trudi, regaining her footing. Tell me about Heike!

Yes, Rolph said. She's in the Mews. A man came looking for you. She's alive.

Is she hurt?, said Trudi. I have to find her. I have to find her so I can look for Hans.

Three floors of the building cracked, groaned, cracked again and fell, sending those stranded on the rubble scrambling for their lives. Trudi watched, fascinated, as though it were a film.

Can you take care of her, Rolph said. Before she could ask what he meant, Trudi saw he had addressed this to Frau Engstahl. You aren't dead, Trudi said to Frau Engstahl, who shook her head.

Rolph sat Trudi down again as Frau Engstahl moved away, her coat speckled with blood.

Listen Trudi, Rolph said, I want you to go find Heike, she's in the Allees, the man's name is Strauss, but Hans's train was strafed and bombed. It didn't come back. No one knows what happened to the boys but you must prepare yourself. I'm sorry to tell you like this but who knows what will…what is going to happen. And you are entitled to know this.

Trudi nodded, feeling like a small child. I'm his mother, after all, she managed to say. Rolph gave her a quick hug, then rose and strode back toward the building, toward the rubble and fires.

He's one of them, she said to Frau Engstahl, who had

returned and was now kneeling beside her..

Hush, said Frau Engstahl. Step over here. You're too close to the building.

Frau Engstahl eased Trudi toward the other side of the street, pausing to examine an old woman who was sitting up and coughing, her weight supported by two young girls. Frau Engstahl put a hand on the old woman's back while telling the girls to keep her in a sitting position, not to let her lie down. She told the old woman to try and breathe normally and to relax. That she would be okay. She said all this in a calm voice, as fire and shadow and fire and shadow flickered across her beautiful, soot stained face.

What about the Hessenkirchen?, Trudi asked as Frau Engstahl returned.

They were killed, Frau Engstahl said. Come over here.

She sat Trudi on a small retaining wall and felt her all over for broken bones. Satisfied Trudi was intact, Frau Engstahl sat down beside her, sitting in the tentative way people sit when they are going to get up.

You'll be fine, Frau Meitner, Frau Engstahl said. You're in shock is all. It will wear off. Stay here for a bit and don't move. One of us will find you when everything is under control.

Yes. Thank you, Trudi said. Thank you for everything.

Frau Engstahl hugged her and stood.

How did they die?, Trudi asked.

Instantly, Frau Engstahl said., understanding Trudi was referring to the Hessenkirchen. Crushed. They were sitting beside me. I had leaned down to tie my shoe.

Trudi nodded, feeling her sanity return. The scene in front of her also seemed to have stabilized. There were fewer screams and the building, which was now one half of a building, no longer spewed black smoke as hoses played water into the rooms of apartments which were open to the air.

VI

.1.

Sometimes you walk through your city, Trudi thought as she walked, and it is the real city, the city you know; and sometimes you walk and it's an imaginary or remembered city. And while most of the time the you who walks through the city is you, at times it's someone else, someone who has appropriated your body to their own purposes, the way the bombers appropriate our city to their purposes. You can't bomb a city without there first being one, just as you can't replace a self unless one already exists. The Self has to exist. Only then can you obliterate it.

As she walked, Trudi realized with certainty that Rolph had told her Hans was dead. As the realization sank in, but the word realization doesn't begin to describe what Trudi felt at that moment, it struck her like a blow to the stomach and she had to stop and bend over and catch her breath or she would have fallen down. She would never see Hans again, never touch him, never hear his voice. This was inconceivable.

Yet at other times during her walk, the idea of Hans's death was simply that: an abstract idea. He was dead, the way so many hundreds of millions were dead before him. Dead meant he had died and his physical body was no longer able to reciprocate your movements with its own. But nothing could stop you from remembering the dead person, even if, for the rest of time, that was all you could do. Time of course was the problem. It went forward. Yet if you could stop it at the moment Hans was expected back from Liebenswald, you could continue to live as though, at any moment, he might arrive. All you needed to do was stop time.

At the intersection of Vielenstrasse and Goethestrasse, Trudi turned right and stepped carefully over the tangle of hoses Hitler Youth were using to fight another building fire. There was nothing unusual in this. They did this every night. Trudi thought briefly of asking a Hitler Youth if he knew her son, then decided this was absurd. Why should he? There were thousands of Hitler Youth scattered throughout their City. These particular Youth had been called on to fight fires, while her son had been called on to donate his genetic material to a farm girl. Each had obeyed his orders.

The crowd which normally watched the Hitler Youth fight fires was missing. Perhaps people hadn't yet been allowed to leave their shelters. Or perhaps everyone who would have made up the crowd of spectators had died in the bombing. Either way, tonight, only Trudi and a few other stragglers watched.

A tap on her shoulder made her turn and she found herself peering up at a Hitler Youth. He was very tall with pale, wolf-like eyes. He asked if she was all right and Trudi said, Yes, I think so. Thank you. He said he was worried because she was crying. Only then did Trudi realize that she was crying. The person who had commandeered her body had no idea what that body was doing.

The Hitler Youth told Trudi they had just now been informed that bombing would resume in a matter of minutes. She should therefore find shelter as soon as possible.

Trudi thanked him again and said she would, and the Youth clicked his heels with a puzzled expression, extended his arm and said Heil Hitler.

Once more, Trudi felt that she was walking. The Allees were two blocks away. She had visited them numerous times, often with the children, when the children were little. At Christmas, the occupants, or owners, in the Allees would dress their houses up as gingerbread houses. They would stand at their entrances, costumed in many cases as Kris Klaus, and pass out cider or chocolate, as well as little presents. The multiple Klauses disturbed Heike, who at the time still believed there was a real Kris Klaus. Year after year, Heike would ask which was the real one and year after year, Trudi would explain that these people had dressed up as Kris Klaus to make believe while the real Kris Klaus was flying down on his way from the north pole.

When will he get here? Heike would ask, looking at the false Klauses with suspicion.

He will never get here, Liebschen, Trudi said out loud. He is a fiction, designed to allow adults to play with their children's innocence, while at the same time, being protective of that innocence.

Yes, but when will he get here?

He's not coming, moron, Hans said aloud, in his most exasperated voice. Death apparently had done nothing for Hans's impatience.

Impatience. That had always been Hans's problem. Even as a baby, Hans was impatient, crying for the breast right up to, and beyond, the moment the nipple entered his mouth. Then he would relax, becoming limp and content, as though he had never shed a tear. By then, Trudi was a nervous wreck and whoever was in their vicinity would be staring daggers at this despicable child-abuser.

The pain punched her in the stomach again and Trudi cried out as she bent over to accept it. Funny, she said to herself, gripping her belly. She had given no thought whatsoever to how Hans had died. Had he died suddenly, or did a bullet enter his stomach so that he died in agony? This mattered, of course, but it didn't matter at the moment. What mattered at the moment wasn't his mode of death. Death was what mattered. How you couldn't grasp Death. You could see, and see quite clearly, your tears and snot falling into the white snow, creating as it did small tunnels in the light powder. But you couldn't get to the bottom of what it meant that your son was dead. As if someone you had lived with you all your life had suddenly turned out to be an illusion.

The one thought Trudi felt she wouldn't be able to bear was that her son hadn't seen the plane flying toward him, that he was struck unawares and died without a single moment to reflect on what was about to happen. Trudi knew this was completely irrational. Seeing the plane would have done Hans no good, and perhaps a great deal of harm: to know for the few seconds he had left on earth that he was about to die. What unspeakable terror he would have felt. And yet, for Trudi, bent over, beginning to breathe again, not knowing was much worse.

They had known. The Others. At the very least, they had known they were going away. This was a blessing because your mind needed time to adjust to such profound transitions. To suddenly pass from a state of existence to one of non-existence was too much. It undermined the power of one's soul and bequeathed the problem of what had happened to the living.

Speaking of death, bombs were falling again. Trudi could hear their hollow booms at a distance of some miles, and hear too the ack ack of the anti-aircraft guns. If she'd had a better view of the sky, she would have been able to see tracers carving their way across the star filled night. The tracers went up like fireworks, but kept going and remained in the sky for a long time before burning themselves out. They gave the ground gunners targets and range, so that the ground gunners could fire at the attacking planes. This was a nightly exercise: the planes, the anti-aircraft fire, the bombs, the planes, and on and on and on. You could set your watch by it. No. Not your watch. You couldn't set your watch by it. But it happened every night. You got used to it. Some days, when you were certain it wouldn't touch you, you might silently enjoy it, enjoy feeling safe while elsewhere in the City...Trudi shook her head and realized she was screaming with all her might. She felt ashamed. This was something a German woman didn't do, scream like this in public.

When Trudi had calmed a bit, the proximity of the bombs told her to hurry. But the moment she reached the Allees, the pain struck again and doubled her over. Trudi tried to throw up, but couldn't. That was a shame. When she had been able to throw up, it had given her a few seconds of relief. She could retch. However retching wasn't the same. In truth, it was horrible. It was failure. Throwing up you returned to Life. Retching, you had nothing to give, nothing to return to. It was like terrible sex, brutal and unrelieving.

Turning into the Allees, which also, except for the moonlight were completely dark, Trudi allowed herself to sit down in the snow and rest. She had been through a lot for one day. They had just told her her son was dead. And her daughter had been injured. All in the space of a few hours. You could go through the entire war without hearing things like this. She had to stop screaming however. It did absolutely no good to scream. Fortunately, there was no one on the street. The resumption of the air raids, preceded by an encore of air raid sirens, had seen to that. Still, you had to preserve appearances. You had to do this because, without preserving appearances, all that was left was screaming. And you couldn't allow that to be all that was left.

Struggling to her feet, which was difficult, not least because the snow was comfortable, Trudi brushed herself off. She needed to be presentable for the people who had rescued Heike. Otherwise, how would they know she was Heike's mother? If Trudi appeared on their doorstep red eyed from crying, disheveled, with snow all over her skirt and coat…People did that these days; they pretended they were the parents of lost children. Of course, she would have to tell Heike that Hans was dead. But not right away. There was even a chance Hans had escaped. No one had said with certainty he was dead, killed.

She would tell Heike Hans was missing. If Heike asked her where he was missing from, she wouldn't answer. She would just slap her. Trudi began to nod to herself. She would slap her because… because…this wasn't the time for Heike's wisecracks, not with the Russians at their doorstep and Hans, the male of the family, missing and presumed dead. The roar overhead must be from enemy planes. She could look up and see the hundreds of shining silvery missiles diving deeper into her countryside or city-side, waiting to drop their bombs. No. I'm not going to do that, Trudi said. I won't give them the satisfaction. There's no reason for me to look up. The moonlight's on their stomachs for some reason. It should be shining on their backs because the moon is higher than they are and they are lower than the moon. Everyone who pays attention to basic science knows that you cannot fly higher than the moon. It is a physical impossibility, just as coming back from the dead is a physical and moral impossibility, unless you weren't dead in the first place, in which case you wouldn't be coming back from the dead but from a clerical error.

No matter how good they are at keeping records, they can't keep track of everything. They can misspell a name, oh God No, even the most careful of them. Somewhere in here, my hands are frozen, somewhere in here if I can stop crying so I can see, I have, what am I looking for? Somewhere in here, if I can stop crying, I have Heike's address. Somewhere in here is Heike's address, the address of the kind people who took Heike in, and if I can just stop shaking and crying, just for a minute, not even a minute, it won't take more than a few seconds, because I've forgotten the address, although I remembered it a moment ago, a moment ago their address was clear in my mind if I could just stop shaking and crying for one second, and, I pull it out of my pocket, I pull it out of my pocket and read it and then I wouldn't have to not know, OH GOD, where I was going, if I could just stop

.2.

When Trudi appeared on their front stoop, the Strausses, who could see that she was in terrible distress, made her tea laced with brandy and insisted that she, as well as Heike, spend the night with them. The bombing had moved east so there would be no need to repair to the Strauss's cellar. The Meitners could go to bed whenever they liked and wake whenever they woke.

Heike, Frau Strauss was happy to report, had recovered her memory and most of her motor functions. She continued to suffer periodic spells of dizziness when she rose too quickly, which was why Frau Strauss had Heike count to ten before getting up, and ten while up. This seemed to help. Frau Strauss could see Trudi was having trouble absorbing what she was being told, but felt it was important to speak nonetheless. There was nothing, Frau Strauss felt, more calming than the sound of a normal human voice.

During this time, Herr Strauss busied himself making the tea, of course it was ersatz tea, adding brandy, and generally seeing to it that his guests were comfortable. The four of them had settled in the small but charming Strauss sitting room, furnished with yellow damask covered couches and adorned with late nineteenth century landscapes, which Herr Strauss collected. Most of these depicted German mountains and forests in winter. Herr Strauss, his wife informed Trudi, had been a champion cross country skier when he was young, although, Herr Strauss dryly put in, there was little left of this person in the old man they now saw before them.

That must have been wonderful, Trudi remarked, without the slightest notion of what she said. Her attention was focused on a small, varnished oil painting, where heavy boughs appeared about to drop loads of fresh snow onto the snow cover beneath. Two squirrels at the base of the tree gazed hopefully at an acorn which appeared to teeter at the end of one of the boughs. It seemed possible to Trudi that if she stared at the bough long enough, the acorn would drop.

Nonsense, said Frau Strauss. You are still handsome and strong.

He is, Mutti, Heike said. He carried me upstairs by himself.

Trudi nodded and expressed her thanks. She found the sitting room charming. It was how she would have furnished a room for her own elderly parents if she'd had the wherewithal, and if they had let her. The tasseled lampshades bothered her. She would have done away with them. And the porcelain dwarves. These she felt were incongruous in a house which otherwise displayed good taste.

Heike had said something, but Trudi was unable to remember what. Since everyone was looking at her, Trudi remarked as simply as possible on the décor, and said she felt at home here. She mentioned in passing that their own building had just been destroyed but that a friend had found them a place to stay. Their new apartment was in a pre-WW I building in Kreuzberg overlooking Manner Platz, which Trudi had always loved. The apartment belonged to a mathematician her friend Rolph worked with, whose wife, a nurse, was presently at the Front. This meant that both Trudi and Heike would be able to have their own rooms.

Heike, who was sitting beside Trudi, took her mother's hand and held it tight. Trudi squeezed back, wondering why Heike was being so demonstrative. Then it occurred to her. It was because Heike hadn't known their building was gone. Trudi really should have taken Heike aside and told her the moment she came in, but she was too upset to think clearly. On the other hand, the loss of their building would temporarily explain her confusion to Heike and the others.

Herr Strauss had spoken, very gently, smiling at her warmly. Trudi thought she heard some word in his sentence, so she replied, No, as far as she knew, the apartment hadn't ever belonged those, but had been passed down in the mathematician's family from generation to generation. However, even had it once belonged to them, it would be unthinkable to let such a large apartment sit vacant when so many people were now homeless. These days, even a short walk revealed people living in shattered if still standing doorways, sometimes in large cartons furnished with donated rugs and blankets. So while the they may have had the right to be unhappy that their homes had been taken away from them, if they were at all human, they would now be glad their apartments were providing space for people who would otherwise have to live on the street.

Mutti. Mutti, please Mutti, Heike was saying. Please, Mutti, stop talking.

Trudi looked across the sitting room at the small dining room, dominated by a large oval dining table, cherrywood? or was it oak, or perhaps chestnut? Yes, it looked like chestnut, and six chestnut side chairs, their seats upholstered in forest green velvet. A hand painted vase sat dead center, on a crocheted table runner. Trudi felt an overwhelming desire to see the vase close up and walked into the dining room, followed by Frau Strauss, who smiled at Heike in such a way that Heike sat back down.

On the vase were paintings of Zeus abducting a maiden, Diana perhaps, or someone else. Perhaps it was Io. Zeus had abducted so many. Frau Strauss lifted the vase and gently placed it in Trudi's hands. We found this together in the Low Countries, Frau Strauss said. We both thought it was delightful and, to tell you the truth, I found it erotic. I told Arthur my feelings that same night and the next afternoon, there it was, wrapped in pink ribbons, sitting by my side of the hotel bed.

That's quite…, Trudi said, nodding and turning the vase, whose other side depicted Zeus kissing the maiden, now in the process of turning into a tree. Trudi handed the vase back and, without thinking, sat on one of the side chairs. The back was stiff, but she found the seat quite comfortable. Frau Strauss sat beside her. Trudi was silent for a few moments, which she spent trying to make out a series of dark paintings on the far wall. They appeared to be ancestor paintings but Frau Strauss, who must have noted where Trudi's gaze fell, failed to provide a commentary.

I'm sorry I brought them up, Trudi said after a while. No matter what your conversation, they always seem to make their way into it. You can be talking about rocks and they'll come up, paramecium, space flight…

It's all right, my dear, Frau Strauss said. We can see you're upset.

Yes, Trudi said. Normally, I'm rational. Perhaps I'm hyper-rational, but tonight, too much has happened. I feel…Never mind how I feel. You seem like kind people and will make allowances for me, no?

Of course, Frau Strauss said, but there is no need to make

any allowances. You are our guest and we like your daughter, who is a most original child.

Trudi nodded.

You have a son too, we understand, who is in the Hitler Youth?

Yes, Trudi said. Hans.

Hans, is that right?, said Frau Strauss. My brother is named Hans.

If Hans were here, Trudi said, we couldn't avoid talking about them. He felt they were at the bottom of everything.

Many people do, Frau Strauss said, as gently as possible.

When someone did something Hans didn't like, he would call them, you know. Or say they were behaving like them. I would yell at him for it. One cannot go around saying that to people. Not only is it insulting. It's dangerous, Hans, and you cannot do it!

It's the times, Frau Strauss agreed. But there's no need for this any longer.

Trudi blinked, waking in an instant from what she felt was a kind of possession. She gazed at Frau Strauss, seeing her for the first time. Frau Strauss had beautiful clear skin, although she must be near eighty, and clear, sparkling blue eyes, which shone even in this dim light. She wore her gray hair in a loose bun and was dressed simply but expensively, in a tweed suit. A cameo rested on her chest, in the form of a simple profile of a woman who, Trudi believed, must look as Frau Strauss once looked when she was young. Did I take you into this room? Trudi said, standing. I'm very sorry, meine Frau. I'm...You must forgive me.

You've had a difficult day, Frau Meitner, Frau Strauss said, standing along with Trudi. I am going to make up a bed for the two of you. Then you and Heike can go to sleep. Sleep will help.

No, Trudi said. Please don't bother. We're well enough to walk home.

Yes, but you have no home, Frau Strauss said softly, laying a hand on Trudi's arm. You will stay with us tonight.

.3.

The bedroom was upstairs, in a gabled space whose ceiling was the house's steeply canted roof. However, the bedroom was wide enough that it easily held a double bed, a dresser with a mirror, and a small nightstand with both a lamp and a pair of candlesticks for when the electricity went out. The rafters that comprised the roof were painted white but the cross beams were left unpainted, adding to the room's rustic feel. The floor, covered with oriental rugs, was made of planked wood, six inches wide, and crooked, so you knew the house was very old. Perhaps three hundred years. Behind the headboard was a thatch of family photographs it was too dark to make out. And to the left, next to the closet door, was another snow-scape, this one of children sledding toward parents who waited for them at the bottom of a hill.

Heike came out of the bathroom and got quickly into bed. She was wearing what must have been one of Frau Strauss's nightdresses, flannel, with thin vertical white lines breaking the soft green field. Heike shivered as she came into contact with the cold sheets, then scuttled over and gripped Trudi around Trudi's midsection.

Are you okay, Mutti? she asked.

Trudi stroked Heike's hair. Yes. I'm fine, she replied.

The other nightdress is for you, Heike said, indicating a red flannel garment with no stripes.

I don't look good in red, Trudi said, still stroking Heike. Is there any other color?

Heike was about to admonish her, but realized in time Trudi was just kidding.

Were you very scared, Mutti? Heike asked.

When?, Trudi asked, picking up the nightdress and rubbing the well-worn fabric between her fingers.

You know. In the shelter. When the building was hit. Was it really a direct hit, Mutti?

Oh, said Trudi. No. You don't have time to be scared, Lieb-schen. I was a little scared before, when the lights went out, but everything happened so quickly. And then, you just wanted to get out.

How did you get out, Mutti? Did you see anything?

Rolph, our upstairs neighbor, helped me. Or maybe it was I followed people with flashlights. And there were candles. Everyone gathered on the street. That's where I saw Rolph...

Heike was silent a moment, and Trudi stared at the dresser. It was very old and obviously hand carved, probably by a village craftsman, as the drawers were uneven and the hardware placed ever so slightly irregularly, although to an undiscerning eye, it might appear to be straight.

Do you know who was killed, Mutti? Heike asked, interrupting Trudi's study.

No, Trudi said. No, and it's time for us to go to sleep, Heike.

I will. Did you see the Neighbor outside?

Yes. I told you, he....Yes. He was outside, then he went back in to find, to help others. I didn't see him after he told me about...About your accident.

How did he know, Mutti?

Herr Strauss walked over but couldn't find me. Herr Starzinger is our Air Marshal. Now, please let me get up, Heike, so I can go to the bathroom

What about Herr Gruber?

I didn't see him, but he was near the doors as usual. He missed you.

Nothing could happen to Herr Gruber, said Heike. Even if a bomb fell on his head, it wouldn't kill him and he would keep telling jokes and making sure he could survive. What about Frau Brest? Did you see her?

No, said Trudi. I'm going to put on my nightdress. I...

What about...

Enough!, Trudi said, standing.

Frau Engstahl?, Heike finished.

She...Frau Engstahl got out, Trudi said, remembering now that she had been certain Frau Engstahl would die that night.

I was afraid to ask about her, Heike said, exhaling deeply. I was afraid Frau Engstahl might have been killed. You're sure she was all right, Mutti? Promise me.

Yes, Trudi said, sitting back down. Are you all right, Heike?

I'm all right, Mutti, Heike said. But my head still hurts a little. Here. Feel it.

Heike took Trudi's hand and placed it on the enormous bump

over on the left side of her cranium. Trudi gasped and felt the bump all over before taking her hand away.

Did a doctor look at you?

Herr Strauss is a doctor, Mutti. He looked at it and said I would be fine.

Trudi shivered, felt the bump once more, kissed Heike, and stood. I'll be right back, she said, tucking the blankets around Heike's sides.

.4.

The bathroom was old fashioned, to be expected in a house of this age, but everything worked. And the more Trudi examined its fixtures and cabinets, and thought about the way the space was arranged, the more she felt great care had gone into the building and the restoring of it. Someone had enclosed the stand-up sink with an oval cabinet so that the cabinet shape echoed the oval shape of the claw foot tub. The rows of small, light blue tile on the wall behind the bathtub were done in irregular lines, to imitate the movement of waves. The bath mat too was cut in the shape of a wave, rising in the middle and falling away on the sides.

Trudi couldn't turn on a light yet as the All Clear hadn't sounded, but there was enough moonlight pouring in through the small frosted glass window that she could see herself in the antique mirror. She looked ghastly, but also, to her great relief, sane. Below the mirror was a small shelf and on the shelf, around the soap dish, on which was a fresh bar of soap, were porcelain miniatures of the Fuhrer, the Reichfuhrer, the Air Marshal, and Eva Braun. The four were placed in such a way that they appeared to be regarding the bar of soap which rested in the carved dish. The Fuhrer had his hands on his hips, in what was a characteristic pose. The Reichfuhrer was polishing a pair of glasses. The Air Marshal was portrayed with his hands over his huge belly as he gazed down at the soap. Only Eva Braun seemed relaxed, one hand pointing at the soap, while her head was thrown back , laughing.

You could tell right away that the porcelains must have been commissioned. No one made porcelains like these. The Strausses must have had them made to order, so that they would surround the soap dish in the second floor bathroom. Trudi remembered with a thrill of dread that she had spoken frankly about them with Frau Strauss, but no matter how hard she tried, she couldn't remember what she had said. She didn't think it was anything incriminating. Besides, she had obviously had a shock and wasn't in her right mind when she arrived. The Strausses would understand that.

Trudi turned on the hot water and, to her surprise, water

poured from the spigot. Warm water. She gathered some in her palms and splashed her face. The moment her face came in contact with the water, she gasped and doubled over again and had to wait a moment for the wave of pain to pass. During that moment, when she ceased breathing, she wouldn't have been surprised if her heart had stopped altogether. But it didn't and Trudi was able to rise, turn off the water, and dry her face on a fresh towel, whose presence was also a small miracle.

The thing to do, she decided as she replaced the towel, was not to think she would never see Hans again, but simply to think she wouldn't see him today. She would wake each morning and tell herself she wouldn't see him today. She wouldn't think about the next day. She would get up and make Heike breakfast, assuming they had food, and prepare for the day when she and Heike would begin to travel West, as Rolph said they would need to once the Russians broke through. It wasn't totally clear how she would prepare for this trip. Resole her shoes? Trudi laughed. This was next to impossible. Every bit of leather in the entire country now went to the war effort. Besides, she and Heike had good shoes. She had put aside two pairs and they would have to do.

Anyway, that lay in the future and the future was exactly what she had determined not to think about. She had washed her face. Now she would pee, change into the nightdress, and go to bed. It occurred to Trudi that she should have peed first, but she could always wash her hands again, once she was finished. No one would tell her not to. From the time they were able to understand her, she would tell the children that they always had to wash their hands after they went to the bathroom, but it had been years and years, she reflected, as she looked out the bathroom window, since anyone had told her what to do.

THE END

Made in the USA
Las Vegas, NV
13 May 2021